NEW PENGUIN SHAKESPEARE

GENERAL EDITOR: T. J. B. SPENCER

ASSOCIATE EDITOR: STANLEY WELLS

WILLIAM SHAKESPEARE

*

MACBETH

**EDITED BY
G. K. HUNTER**

PENGUIN BOOKS

PENGUIN BOOKS

Published by the Penguin Group
Penguin Books Ltd, 27 Wrights Lane, London W8 5TZ, England
Penguin Putnam Inc., 375 Hudson Street, New York, New York 10014, USA
Penguin Books Australia Ltd, Ringwood, Victoria, Australia
Penguin Books Canada Ltd, 10 Alcorn Avenue, Toronto, Ontario, Canada M4V 3B2
Penguin Books (NZ) Ltd, Private Bag 102902, NSMC, Auckland, New Zealand

Penguin Books Ltd, Registered Offices: Harmondsworth, Middlesex, England

This edition first published in Penguin Books 1967
Reprinted with revised Further Reading and Account of the Text 1995
48

Printed in England by Clays Ltd, St Ives plc
Set in Monotype Ehrhardt

CONTENTS

INTRODUCTION

THE SENSE OF THE PLAY

REDUCED to its plot-line, *Macbeth* sounds like a crime-does-not-pay melodrama. The lady who, in the Thurber story, saw it in Penguin Books and supposed that it must be a whodunit, need not have been so violently disillusioned: 'I got real comfy in bed that night and all ready to read a good mystery story, and here I had *The Tragedy of Macbeth* – a book for high-school students, like *Ivanhoe.*' *Macbeth* is in fact far more a crime story than a costume melodrama like *Ivanhoe*. But as a crime-does-not-pay story it is less concerned with the uncovering of the crime to others than with the uncovering of the criminal *to himself.* The play spreads out from our interest in the hero; and the hero is here a criminal, or rather a man obsessed by his relation to those criminal tendencies that are so universal that we best describe them by speaking of 'evil'. The play is a discovery or anatomy of evil. Of all Shakespeare's plays *Macbeth* is the one most obsessively concerned with evil. Of course, evil men had appeared in Shakespeare's plays before 1606 – Aaron the Moor, for example, Don John, Shylock, Claudius, Iago, Edmund – but in each of these cases the evil was a shadow placed amid sunlight, beside the radiance of Desdemona, Cordelia, Beatrice or the suffering-for-good of Titus and Othello. Here the evil is, for once and without doubt, larger, more fascinating, more effective than the pallid representation of good (III.2.52–3):

> *Good things of day begin to droop and drowse,*
> *Whiles night's black agents to their preys do rouse.*

7

Macbeth falls, but does not do so primarily because of the processes or power of his enemies. His black tyranny produces the engines of its own destruction; the movement that carries Malcolm, Macduff and Seyward above him is generated first by his own downward tendency and only secondarily by their efforts.

The pallid quality of Malcolm and the other 'good' men of this play is not, however, to be seen simply as Shakespeare's failure to produce radiance. Humility and self-distrust – even self-effacement – are necessary antitheses to the qualities of evil, as this work displays them. E. M. W. Tillyard puts this effectively: Malcolm is 'the ideal ruler who has subordinated all personal pleasures, and with them all personal charm, to his political obligations' (*Shakespeare's History Plays*, p. 317). Good struggles forward in the world of *Macbeth*; but evil is all-pervasive. The whole land lies under its interdict; good men die or fly; but even in flight they cannot escape from its power. They are walled up in the suspiciousness of the isolated individual. They do not know what other men may mean, or what is true or false; 'fair' may be 'foul'; they must guard their own tongues.

Act IV, scene 3 (the long scene of testing in the English court), can be viewed, in this respect, as the turning-point of the play, since there the suspiciousness, the sense that the individual cannot move directly, gradually gives way before the knowledge of mutual dependence, of national identity, and of divine blessing. Sharing comes as a kind of holy cure for suffering. The *malaise* that has spread from Macbeth into his subjects and even into his enemies, the inability to trust another, the need to conceal thoughts, to

> *look like the innocent flower,*
> *But be the serpent under't . . .*

as Lady Macbeth says (I.5.63-4), is checked here; and in the following scenes the plague is gradually driven back to the single castle and the single man. Only when he is dead, his head on a pole, is 'The time . . . free'.

If Malcolm is 'the medicine of the sickly weal' Macbeth is its disease – a point the imagery is constantly making. One of the difficulties of approaching Macbeth is that he is seen so roundedly and so simultaneously as a social and a psychological disease. His infection spreads outside his own mind and into the minds of others. At the same time, he is himself the first victim, though thereafter (like the werewolf) the victimizer.

If we call Macbeth a victim we will wish to know how he was first infected; and this is one of the crucial questions of the play. This question also requires to be tackled on the social no less than the psychological plane. When we first hear of Macbeth he is a great warrior, marvellously steeped in blood (I.2.40-42):

> *Except they meant to bathe in reeking wounds . . .*
> *I cannot tell.*

The stage-horror of the messenger's account of the extraordinarily bloody series of battles in Act I is being used at the explicit level to suggest that Macbeth is a hero. But I think that we are also aware (and meant to be aware) that this horrifying potentiality (even *penchant*) for destruction is held inside human morality only by bonds of loyalty that are easy to snap – witness the exemplary first Thane of Cawdor, whose inheritor Macbeth becomes (I.2.70):

> *What he hath lost, noble Macbeth hath won.*

Macbeth begins in frightening loyalty (like a wild animal on a lead). Shakespeare makes nothing of his genuine and legal claim to the throne (as it appears in Holinshed's

Chronicles, where he found the story) - an explanation if not an excuse for his action; but he does seem to suggest that the succession was not finally settled when Macbeth arrived back in court in Act I, scene 4. And it is only then that Duncan announces (lines 38-40):

> *We will establish our estate upon*
> *Our eldest, Malcolm, whom we name hereafter*
> *The Prince of Cumberland. . . .*

Duncan's sudden act here (it was not expected by 'cousin' Macbeth) has something of the same wilful arbitrariness as Lear's division of his kingdom. But one must not make this point to 'excuse' Macbeth's subsequent actions. I take it that the function of these early hints is to stress the uncertainty of loyalty as a controlling counterweight to violence and bloodthirstiness. Once loose this man on society, the early scenes seem to be saying, and he will not stop 'Even till destruction sicken'.

We must add to the uncertainty of the social sanctions that hold Macbeth in place a corresponding uncertainty about psychological restraint. The wife who knows him best tells us (I.5.19-23) that he is one who

> *wouldst not play false,*
> *And yet wouldst wrongly win. Thou'dst have, great Glamis,*
> *That which cries, 'Thus thou must do' if thou have it,*
> *And that which rather thou dost fear to do*
> *Than wishest should be undone.*

That is, Macbeth *fears* to do evil; but what he fears is the image of himself committing the evil deed, rather than the evil deed itself. What is startling by its absence from this moral landscape is any sense of positive *love* for good, any sense of personal involvement in virtue, loyalty, restraint.

Here, as on the social plane, the power of Macbeth (*ambition* here rather than bloodthirstiness) is presented as free-floating, with only the weakest of psychological restraints attached, and with powerful enemies of restraint (like Lady Macbeth) dedicated (quite literally) to its destruction. And in such a miasma of undirected power, free-floating will-lessness, 'Fair is foul', 'the battle's lost and won', indecision has the only decisive victory.

But *Macbeth* does not finally chronicle the triumphs of indecision. Evil does not become alive or actual until it is endorsed by the *will*, say the moral theologians, and so it is in *Macbeth*. The play begins with the Witches, and the Witches must be supposed to be evil; but the mode of evil they can create is potential only, not actual, till the human agent takes it inside his mind and makes it his own by a motion of the will. This is demonstrated in the play in two ways; firstly by the tale the First Witch tells of her utmost malice – the tale of the 'master o'the *Tiger*' (I.3.18–25):

> *I'll drain him dry as hay;*
> *Sleep shall neither night nor day*
> *Hang upon his penthouse lid.*
> *He shall live a man forbid.*
> *Weary sev'n-nights nine times nine*
> *Shall he dwindle, peak, and pine.*
> *Though his bark cannot be lost,*
> *Yet it shall be tempest-tossed.*

The history of the 'master o'the *Tiger*' is a preview of the history of another 'pilot . . . | Wracked as homeward he did come' – of Macbeth. Macbeth too will be drained as dry as hay (morally rather than physically) but his bark *will* be lost, because he scuttles it himself.

The other, and far more important, demonstration of the Witches' evil as potential rather than actual appears in the contrast of Macbeth and Banquo. 'Our captains, Macbeth and Banquo' are coupled in the King's mouth as approximate equals, and there is no suggestion that one is superior in rank to the other. They are alike in dignity and in bravery; the Witches salute both of them. The essential difference appears in response to the salute.

> ... why do you start, and seem to fear
> Things that do sound so fair?

says Banquo to his partner (I.3.50–51). Thus Innocence greets Guilt. It is not that Banquo is innocent of the knowledge of Evil: he recognizes the Witches for what they are – 'The instruments of darkness' – but he sees his own role as requiring him to combat this something external, since (lines 122–5)

> oftentimes, to win us to our harm,
> The instruments of darkness tell us truths;
> Win us with honest trifles, to betray's
> In deepest consequence.

Banquo recognizes the evil and sees it as something threatening, but outside himself. Macbeth, as soon as he can speak apart from his fellows, unfolds a different reaction (I.3.133–41):

> why do I yield to that suggestion
> Whose horrid image doth unfix my hair,
> And make my seated heart knock at my ribs
> Against the use of nature? Present fears
> Are less than horrible imaginings.
> My thought, whose murder yet is but fantastical,
> Shakes so my single state of man
> That function is smothered in surmise,
> And nothing is but what is not.

'Suggestion' is a technical term of theology, meaning 'a prompting or incitement to evil; a temptation of the Evil One'; it is a thing in itself external; but Macbeth finds the stability of his moral nature already yielding, already 'moved'. In terms of his physical nature, his 'fixed' hair and his 'seated' heart leave their appointed places; his 'single state of man', his little kingdom of human faculties, finds its functioning 'smothered' by the tingling horror-pleasure of anticipated evil. The suggestion of the Witches 'starts' Macbeth (in more senses than one) because it finds an answering image inside his own mind. 'Macbeth has already contemplated the murder,' say literal-minded critics. Whether or not this is so seems not to be a crucial point in terms of the view of evil that the play contains; for (as Milton later announces)

> Evil into the mind of God or Man
> May come and go, so unapprov'd, and leave
> No spot or blame behind. . . .

Adam is here speaking of Eve's dream, and he goes on

> Which gives me hope
> That what in sleep thou didst abhor to dream
> Waking thou never wilt consent to do.
> Paradise Lost, V.117–121

This view of evil is precisely endorsed later in *Macbeth* (II.1.8–9) when Banquo begs the 'Merciful powers' to

> Restrain in me the cursèd thoughts that nature
> Gives way to in repose.

Banquo, no less than Macbeth, may have contemplated murder in this 'natural' way of allowing the thought to pass through his mind. But he recognizes such 'cursèd thoughts' for what they are, as he recognized the 'instruments of darkness' – and not simply in terms of intellectual recognition, but by a positive and almost sensory reaction to the 'smell' of evil. Macbeth's sensory reactions, on the other hand, point not to a direct and uncompromising rejection of evil, but to a paralysis of the moral powers.

I spoke earlier of Macbeth's gift for bloodshed, and his ambition, as 'free-floating' qualities which were, in themselves, neither good nor bad, but as the direction of their use made them so. Ambition to excel as an obedient general, bloodthirstiness in the destruction of national foes – these are insulated from evil by loyal intent. But the Witches hold up a mirror in which Macbeth sees his powers fulfilled in a quite contrary way, and the fear-and-joy that this evokes in him is such that he cannot wrench his will into a denial. He is 'possessed' by the image of himself that the Witches show; and though he can respond to Banquo's description of the external appearance created by this 'possession' ('Look how our partner's rapt') with the commonplaces of external morality (I.3.143–4):

If chance will have me king, why chance may crown me
Without my stir

and

Come what come may,
Time and the hour runs through the roughest day,

nevertheless the effect is that of a man gradually waking out of a dream, a dream that turns the 'reality' of social obligations and social chat into a rigmarole of play-acting. His life hereafter is increasingly to be eaten up by this dream-self, by this 'new' Macbeth springing up within him and making the normal motions of his conventional self sound like 'a tale | Told by an idiot . . . Signifying nothing'.

Macbeth, coming out of the dream of fulfilled ambition that the Witches show him, comes back into a world of shared responsibilities and paternal affection, so luminously benevolent, so joyfully held together – even at the point of the traitor Cawdor's execution – that the dream seems impossible even to speak about (and Macbeth and his Lady speak about it, in fact, only by periphrasis or euphemism). His real affection for his King and for his wife intertwine in his journey to prepare a welcome in Inverness. The individual will-to-good is paralysed (or anaesthetized) inside him; but the sense of social obligations and virtues seems to remain entire – like a rotten apple with an unblemished skin. Inverness Castle still looks like 'a pleasant seat', Lady Macbeth like a 'most kind hostess', Macbeth like a 'worthiest cousin' and, strangest of all (I.7.17–20), Duncan like a king who

> hath been
> *So clear in his great office, that his virtues*
> *Will plead like angels, trumpet-tongued against*
> *The deep damnation of his taking-off.*

Lady Macbeth's function in the destruction of Macbeth is (ironically enough) to push the 'new' Macbeth that the Witches' 'suggestion' has tempted Macbeth into accepting, right through the smiling surface of the social scene (to which she belongs), to translate the anaesthetized lack of will-to-good into a positive (and fatal) evil action (I.7.35–6, 39–41).

> *Was the hope drunk*
> *Wherein you dressed yourself? . . . Art thou afeard*
> *To be the same in thine own act and valour*
> *As thou art in desire?*

Macbeth knows that he can give no reasons for acting in the way thus proposed (I.7.25–8):

> *I have no spur*
> *To prick the sides of my intent but only*
> *Vaulting ambition which o'erleaps itself*
> *And falls on the other.*

But in *his* sleep-walking scene (Act II, scene 1) he needs no more than her impulsion (weak in itself) to move the whole passive weight of his will-less power into frightening action. As the visionary dagger moves without force towards Duncan's bedchamber, so does the envisioning Macbeth.

The impulse comes from Lady Macbeth, I have said, and the actual performance is Macbeth's; but in no real sense is this a shared action. Lady Macbeth is willing to make it so: her 'Consider it not so deeply', her 'My husband!', her

> *Why, worthy thane,*
> *You do unbend your noble strength*

for example, are direct invitations to shared guilt; but Macbeth's replies, his 'Methought I heard a voice cry, "Sleep no more!" ', his 'There's one did laugh in's sleep', his 'But wherefore could not I pronounce "Amen"?' and so on are like cries of terror from one half of his nature to the other, from the new Macbeth to the old, for reassurance:

> *To know my deed 'twere best not know myself.*

The essential dialogue here is with himself; and Lady Macbeth, like other people in the play, remains accessory merely. The deed is done, for reasons that he does not understand; the rest of his life is the attempt to live with the deed as well as the self that his social existence might seem to imply. The deed itself is a denial of all social obligations, all sharing, all community of feeling, even with his wife; but it is only gradually that the complete divorce between self and society is realized and accepted, where realization means total sterility, and acceptance requires moral death.

Macbeth's bringing of his world into conformity with the man that he has become is the process I described at the beginning of this Introduction in terms of a social disease. It is not a process that he self-consciously undertakes as a practical programme. He thinks of himself as a part of the social order, as a man married, ruling, leading those willing to be led; but the hollowness of the order that he can encompass forces him backwards all the time into the total isolation that is his 'natural' milieu.

Thus in the banquet scene (Act III, scene 4) and in the scenes associated with it (Act III, scenes 1 and 2) Macbeth acts as a man still seeking a social good, a good that only needs the deaths of Banquo and Fleance to make it click into place. In fact, the death of Banquo alters nothing important, and the escape of Fleance is seen not as the one chance that spoils an otherwise perfect piece of kingship, but rather as a type of the future that always eludes (and must elude) the grasp of the tyrannical present. Macbeth operates throughout all these scenes by incessant falsehood or prevarication. With considerable skill he extracts from Banquo, in the stream of his false flattery, the basic facts necessary for the murder. He lies to the assembled Lords when he welcomes them and pretends hospitality. There is no reason to suppose he is not lying to the Murderers when he tells them that Banquo is their enemy. He certainly lies in his pretence of trusting them; for why else does he plant the Third Murderer in their midst? He will not even trust his wife, as he makes clear with grim joviality (III.2.45-6):

> *Be innocent of the knowledge, dearest chuck,*
> *Till thou applaud the deed.*

The gap that the deed has made, even between its two accomplices, is obvious here. Lady Macbeth's

> *Why do you keep alone . . . ?*
> *Things without all remedy*
> *Should be without regard ; what's done is done*

(III.2.8-12) is painfully irrelevant to the real situation of Macbeth's mind. It may be true that what's done is done; but the man new-made by the deed is still alive, and cannot be 'without regard'. This is Macbeth's problem; he cannot forget the deed; for that would be to forget himself. He has become 'the deed's creature' so completely that the only movement he can make is towards the sterility of total identification with his deed (III.4.135-7):

> *I am in blood*
> *Stepped in so far, that, should I wade no more,*
> *Returning were as tedious as go o'er.*

But in the banquet scene itself the first thing that must impress us is the skill with which host and hostess can collaborate to establish a show of order and conviviality. It is impressive, but, as Murderer and Ghost indicate, far from reality. Moreover, the banquet here is bound to remind us of the earlier banquet, in Act I, scene 7, where a real order still existed, surrounding the benevolent Duncan

> *shut up*
> *In measureless content,*

where Macbeth himself, skulking outside the door, was the only breach in nature. And we should also be reminded of Duncan's lines about Macbeth (I.4.55-7):

> *he is full so valiant,*
> *And in his commendations I am fed;*
> *It is a banquet to me.*

Our sense of 'banqueting' in the play has moved a long way from this.

The bloodstained Murderer should also cast his shadow backwards – to the bleeding Captain in Act I, scene 2. But the bleeding Captain brought news of the deaths of enemies; the bloodshed then was open and honourable; and treachery (that of Cawdor) was remote (and past). Now the bloodstained messenger cannot be openly acknowledged; for the blood upon his face is that of Banquo, the 'chief guest', whose absence from the feast is being deplored; treachery is no longer external; indeed it is now the principle by which the court operates.

The banquet scene establishes itself, with dramatic tentacles reaching back to earlier scenes, as a phoney show of order, in which Macbeth's 'real' life of bloodshed and treachery seeks to hide behind 'mouth-honour, breath | Which the poor heart would fain deny'. This is a climactic scene because it also establishes, once and for all, that the real world of Macbeth's bloodshed and treachery *cannot* be repressed, nor its dreadful burgeoning halted; it erupts to the surface inconveniently enough in the First Murderer; but catastrophically when the Ghost of Banquo enters to claim the royal seat that his children are going to inherit. The surface of mutual congratulation is shattered. The scene may begin with: 'You know your own degrees, sit down' – a paradigm of order – but it soon emerges (III.4. 108-9) that

>   *You have displaced the mirth, broke the good meeting*
>   *With most admired disorder.*

And it ends (lines 118–19) with something like a rout of the social virtues:

>   *Stand not upon the order of your going;*
>   *But go at once.*

One of the most effective theatrical points in the whole play occurs here. The coda of the scene shows us the King and Queen, now alone, slumped in their finery amid the debris of the 'great feast', while guilt, horror and relentless resolution pass before their minds. Lady Macbeth, exhausted by the terrible events just passed and by the effort to cover up for her husband, never really re-establishes herself. She is never again to be capable of the resolution that we have seen here and heretofore; she has drawn out all the stops that she knows; she has used again the supreme taunt of effeminacy, which was so effective before the murder; but here it has had only limited success. True, Macbeth has recovered his poise, and the Ghost has vanished; but the recovery has been in terms that establish his psychological power over himself only at the expense of his social ruin. Her success excludes herself from the recovery, for Macbeth no longer needs her. He climbs out of his abyss by planning new exploits, by action which needs no pondering (III.4.138–9):

>   *Strange things I have in head, that will to hand;*
>   *Which must be acted ere they may be scanned.*

Life still offers a future, for there are still people to be murdered – Macduff for example – and this is enough to keep him going. With appalling clarity he now accepts the Witches for what they are – 'the worst' – and knows the course that lies in front of him (lines 134–5):

> *For mine own good*
>
> *All causes shall give way.*

Having faced up to, and named, his fate, he is ready to face
the Witches again.

Act IV, scene 1, differs from the earlier Witch-scenes in
a number of ways. Macbeth now seeks out the Witches on
his own account; and he is now an adept seeking physical
details of the future rather than the innocent, susceptible
of moral shock, that rode across the heath in Act I,
scene 3. He knows that his success is being bought by
damnation, and he does not care. All he cares about is
'security' in what he does; in that case moral status becomes irrelevant; for then (III.4.20–22) he is

> *perfect,*
> *Whole as the marble, founded as the rock,*
> *As broad and general as the casing air. . . .*

But what is 'security'? Hecat reminds us (III.5.32–3) that

> *you all know security*
> *Is mortals' chiefest enemy.*

This is a useful reminder, for the word is one that has lost
its relevant meaning. The *Oxford English Dictionary* tells
us that it is '*archaic :* a culpable absence of anxiety'. The
absence of anxiety was conceived to be culpable, because
man may not be confident or 'secure' about the most important thing in life - his salvation. If he is 'secure', then
it must be because the Devil has closed up his senses to the
obvious and omnipresent dangers that everyone knew to
lurk around the living - because he is in that state of sad-
ness that theologians called 'despair'. An Elizabethan
Morality play makes these points abundantly clear to us,
and throws a flood of light on the second half of *Macbeth*.

It is called *The Cradle of Security*. The text has perished, but the preacher R. Willis recalled, towards the end of his life, having seen a performance of it in Gloucester, in some year around 1570:

> *My father took me with him and made me stand between his legs, as he sat upon one of the benches where we saw and heard very well. The play was called 'The Cradle of Security', wherein was personated a king or some great prince, with his courtiers of several kinds, amongst which three ladies were in special grace with him; and they, keeping him in delights and pleasures, drew him from his graver counsellors, hearing of sermons, and listening to good counsel and admonitions, that in the end they got him to lie down in a cradle upon the stage, where these three ladies, joining in a sweet song, rocked him asleep, that he snorted again; and in the meantime closely conveyed under the clothes wherewithal he was covered a vizard like a swine's snout upon his face, with three wire chains fastened thereunto, the other end whereof being holden severally by those three ladies, who fall to singing again, and then discovered his face, that the spectators might see how they had transformed him, going on with their singing. Whilst all this was acting, there came forth of another door at the farthest end of the stage two old men, the one in blue with a sergeant-at-arms's mace on his shoulder, the other in red with a drawn sword in his hand, and leaning with the other hand upon the other's shoulder. And so they two went along in a soft pace round about by the skirt of the stage, till at last they came to the cradle, when all the court was in greatest jollity; and then the foremost old man with his mace struck a fearful blow upon the cradle, whereat all the courtiers, with the three ladies and the vizard all vanished; and the desolate prince, starting up bare-faced, and finding himself thus sent*

for to judgement, made a lamentable complaint of his miser-
able case, and so was carried away by wicked spirits. This
prince did personate in the moral, the wicked of the world;
the three ladies, Pride, Covetousness, and Luxury; the two
old men, the end of the world and the Last Judgement. This
sight took such impression in me, that when I came towards
man's estate, it was as fresh in my memory as if I had seen
it newly acted.

It is in such a cradle that the Witches rock Macbeth in the
second half of the play. They assure him that whatever he
does, he has nothing to fear (IV.1.78–80):

> *Be bloody, bold, and resolute; laugh to scorn*
> *The power of man; for none of woman born*
> *Shall harm Macbeth.*

A man less desperately secure than Macbeth might question that 'power of *man*', for the evil-doer had, traditionally,
more to fear from God than from man; but the desperate
man is in no condition to make moral discriminations. He
grasps at every straw: he knows that the future can hold
nothing for him; but he must act as if he could plan ahead
meaningfully. And murder remains a meaningful activity
even when other human possibilities have faded away
(IV.1.149–52):

> *The castle of Macduff I will surprise,*
> *Seize upon Fife, give to the edge o' the sword*
> *His wife, his babes, and all unfortunate souls*
> *That trace him in his line.*

Act IV is made up of two contrasting glimpses into the
future and two contrary journeys in search of security or
reassurance. Macbeth journeys to the hovel of the Witches
for assurance that he need not fear the future. Macduff

travels to the English court to find hope, to seek a cure for
the horror of the recent past. The 'testing' of Macduff is
in contrast to Macbeth's attempt to question the powers
that speak to him: in one case the mistrust that separates
men is removed by the testing; in the other case, the questions lead only further into the fog of self-deception; and
at the end of Act IV, scene 1, when the Witches vanish,
Macbeth is more alone than ever:

> *Where are they? Gone! Let this pernicious hour*
> *Stand aye accursèd in the calendar. . . .*
> *Infected be the air whereon they ride,*
> *And damned all those that trust them.*

He is left clutching the Witches' promise – his 'charm' as
Macduff calls it – and (in spite of himself) depending on
it; for he has nothing else to depend on. The court of
Edward the Confessor, in contrast to the Witches' hovel,
is a place of holy arts. The only charms used are 'holy
prayers', and the effect is to cure

> *strangely visited people,*
> *All swollen and ulcerous, pitiful to the eye. . . .*

The Witches 'infect' where they ride, but King Edward
disinfects. Macbeth promises evil, and performs it before
the promise is well out of his mouth: Malcolm promises
evil, but never even dreams of performing it. King Edward
has a 'heavenly gift of prophecy'; the prophetic powers of
the Witches come from hell. Macduff's suffering for the
loss of his children is a measure of his true humanity,
measured by his involvement in the sufferings of others
(IV.3.220–26):

> *I must also feel it as a man.*
> *I cannot but remember such things were*
> *That were most precious to me. . . . Sinful Macduff!*

24

They were all struck for thee. Naught that I am,
Not for their own demerits, but for mine,
Fell slaughter on their souls.

Macbeth, on the other hand, has come to measure 'manliness' by the absence of feelings, as his wife had earlier instructed him to; and when his wife dies he can neither remember with gratitude nor look forward to 'things . . . | That were most precious to me.' Throughout the last Act, up to the episode of his death, he has his 'security', his assurance that he will not die by 'one of woman born'. But the enemies that he has to contend with are not ones that can be dealt with by arms or by the strength of a fortress. He puts his armour on long before it is required; but within his impregnable fortress we see his wife fall, before a foe that cannot be resisted - her own conscience; he cannot put an armour on her heart. Despair, which has turned him to stone, has turned her to water, imprisoned her forever in the horror of the past; with the only obvious escape-route running through suicide. Death walks the battlements of Dunsinane in many forms, and few of them involve the official enemy from England. The castle, whose stony strength resembles that of Macbeth himself, immobile in despair, is (like his 'sere [and] yellow leaf') in clear contrast to the 'leavy screen' from Birnan Wood which Malcolm's soldiers take up to protect them as they travel through the country, and then throw down again; just as his fixed posture of 'valiant fury' contrasts with the humility and tentativeness of their hold on the future: 'Let our just censures,' says Macduff, 'Attend the true event'; and Seyward takes up the same point (V.4.19–20):

Thoughts speculative their unsure hopes relate,
But certain issue strokes must arbitrate. . . .

They rely on the future to fulfil their hopes; he knows that the future cannot differ from the present: 'I have lived long enough. . . . Life's but a walking shadow . . . I 'gin to be aweary of the sun.'

It is interesting to note that in the last Act-and-a-half the name 'Macbeth' is little used; he is 'the tyrant', 'the confident tyrant'; this loss of personal identity and assimilation to the type of 'the tyrant' is in keeping with the general movement of the play. Within the castle we witness the atrophy of hope, of the sense of a personal future. Macbeth here is like those 'betrayers of their lords' that Dante finds frozen in the rigid silence of the bottom of Hell, iced-up in despair. Outside, in the army of Malcolm, we see the same facts from a more social point of view: a disease has to be plucked out of the body politic. And this is certainly one of the leading effects made at the end of the play. 'The time is free', the 'dead butcher and his fiend-like queen' have been properly disposed of. Yet the ending is not couched simply in these social terms. The final exchange between Macbeth and Macduff points at a more complex valuation. Macbeth's refusal to fight with Macduff because

>*my soul is too much charged*
>*With blood of thine already*

(V.6.44–5) is unexpected and (no doubt) implausible in terms of real-life psychology. But the idea of a 'good' Macbeth, buried somewhere beneath the activities of a will dedicated to evil, has not been allowed to perish altogether at any point in the play. The fact that 'the tyrant' can describe, so movingly (V.3.24–5),

>*that which should accompany old age,*
>*As honour, love, obedience, troops of friends*

while stressing that he cannot have these things, is sufficient to point to us the wasted potentialities behind the wicked actuality. And so with the final unwillingness to fight Macduff. Macbeth is a man, not a fiend. Motions of the will tending to good still fluctuate round the hardened heart, though they are powerless to affect the general disposition of his will, or to undo what has been done. The same may be said of the brief *anagnorisis*, the sudden moment of total recognition of what the 'juggling fiends' have done – when he draws back from Macduff and says 'I'll not fight with thee.' It is not a moment that can be expanded: time is irreversible; Macbeth has become 'the tyrant' and his fate in life is to be exhibited as 'the tyrant'. What the force of his vitality (that *sine qua non* of heroism) has turned into is a power to accept whatever is necessary, to die with harness on his back; and so he dies, as he began the play, fighting manfully. But without the flinching, without the moment of *anagnorisis*, the final heroic resistance would not be fully human, and if Macbeth was not fully human we would not be interested enough to do more than detest him. As it is, we detest not so much what he *is*, as what he has become, the *process* of damnation.

The same point might be made, in rather more conventional terms, by pointing out that 'Macbeth is a poet'. This is, of course, a dangerous over-simplification. It is Shakespeare who is the poet, and any assumption that Macbeth himself has 'a poetic temperament' (whatever that may be) would be notable false psychology. But it is true that the play's poetic energy contrives to centre on Macbeth, right to the end. And the poetic temper of the play is one that is particularly appropriate to Macbeth. The rhythms have a new fluency for Shakespearian verse, suitable to the rapid and violent change of focus and interest that characterizes his thought. There is a sense of barely suppressed impatience or violence in the disjunction of image from

27

image, thought from thought, phrase from phrase as may be seen in the following (III.2.45-55):

> Be innocent of the knowledge, dearest chuck,
> Till thou applaud the deed. Come, seeling night,
> Scarf up the tender eye of pitiful day,
> And with thy bloody and invisible hand
> Cancel and tear to pieces that great bond
> Which keeps me pale. Light thickens
> And the crow makes wing to the rooky wood;
> Good things of day begin to droop and drowse,
> Whiles night's black agents to their preys do rouse.
> Thou marvell'st at my words; but hold thee still.
> Things bad begun make strong themselves by ill.

The imagery of the play is very notable and has often been commented upon; it, likewise, is lurid and violent – 'shapes of horror, dimly seen in the murky air or revealed by the glare of the cauldron' (as Bradley says). Darkness, blood, fire, the reverberation of noise like thunder, the world of the actor, of the man wearing clothes that are too grand for him – these are continuously invoked to give us (once again) the sense of an inferno barely controlled beneath the surface crust.

The poetic impression is of a hold on coherence which is tossed and distorted by inner violence and destructiveness, nearly broken up by the pressures upon it, but which survives, however narrowly; and this spills over to affect our impression of Macbeth himself. His mind, likewise, is distorted by violence and terror; and though there is nothing morally admirable about the capacity to speak well, we are in fact held sympathetically by a sense of surviving significance in his rhythms, even in those final speeches whose content is devoted to the meaninglessness of existence.

The poetry, in short, carries our sympathy beyond the point where ordinary human identification can expect to operate. We continue to respond to the rhythms of the human heart even when the lives before us are, as Dr Johnson pointed out, 'merely detested'.

THE PLAY IN PERFORMANCE

It is usually supposed today that *Macbeth* was first performed before James I and his royal guest, King Christian IV of Denmark, some time during the latter's visit to England – 17 July to 11 August 1606. It has been argued that the performance took place at Hampton Court on 7 August 1606, one of the three occasions when Shakespeare's company acted before the kings, and this is perfectly possible.

It can also be argued, over and above this, that the play was *written* with James's tastes in mind (see 'Background of the Play', below). If so, it was also (presumably) written with indoor performance in mind, and this would link up with some features of its theatrical technique. A play designed specifically for the afternoon daylight of The Globe might find it hard to give a visual equivalent to the verbal atmosphere of darkness and murk that characterizes *Macbeth*. But a courtly 'nocturnal' could very well project the sense of gloom that the play requires. The play may also have been designed to be spectacular – many court plays were. Apparitions, and such sound effects as thunder, owls, bells, oboes, and trumpets, abound. It is a moot point how the Witches made their exits and entrances. Some kind of 'disappearing trick' seems to be implied for the exit at I.3.77. 'Whither are they vanished?' asks Banquo. Macbeth answers:

> *Into the air; and what seemed corporal*
> *Melted, as breath into the wind.*

Again, Macbeth says in Act IV, scene 1:

> *Infected be the air whereon they ride*

which may be taken to imply flying witches. The Jacobean court masque used elaborate stage-machinery and it may be that *Macbeth* did likewise.

It has been supposed that the last figure in the dumb-show of kings in Act IV, scene 1, who is said in the text to have 'a glass in his hand', represented Mary, Queen of Scots; and used the glass to reflect the figure of James himself, the principal spectator of the play. No doubt it would have been improper to represent James in any other way; but it is difficult to see how the glass operated, or how the audience knew it was operating. Certainly the performances at The Globe must have used a different technique.

Elizabethan and Jacobean court plays were seldom designed only for the court; and *Macbeth*, if the company followed the normal practice, would be played at The Globe soon afterwards. We know that it *was* played at the public theatre, for a record of one such early performance – on 20 April 1611 – has survived among the papers of Dr Simon Forman, an astrologer who kept notes of plays seen, 'for policy': that is, in order to record moral or social lessons that he had learned (the textual implications of Forman's note are discussed on pages 40–41):

In Macbeth, at the Globe, 1610 [mistake for 1611], *the 20th of April* [Saturday], *there was to be observed first how Macbeth and Banquo two noblemen of Scotland, riding through a wood, there stood before them three women fairies or nymphs, and saluted Macbeth, saying three times unto him, Hail, Macbeth, king of Codon, for thou shalt be a king, but shalt beget no kings, &c. Then said Banquo*

What, all to Macbeth and nothing to me? Yes, said the nymphs, Hail, to thee, Banquo; thou shalt beget kings, yet be no king. And so they departed, and came to the Court of Scotland, to Duncan king of Scots, and it was in the days of Edward the Confessor. And Duncan bade them both kindly welcome, and made Macbeth [sic] forthwith Prince of Northumberland, and sent him home to his own castle, and appointed Macbeth to provide for him, for he would sup with him the next day at night, and did so. And Macbeth contrived to kill Duncan, and through the persuasion of his wife did that night murder the king in his own castle, being his guest. And there were many prodigies seen that night and the day before. And when Macbeth had murdered the king, the blood on his hands could not be washed off by any means, nor from his wife's hands, which handled the bloody daggers in hiding them, by which means they became both much amazed and affronted. The murder being known, Duncan's two sons fled, the one to England, the [other to] Wales, to save themselves; they being fled, they were supposed guilty of the murder of their father, which was nothing so. Then was Macbeth crowned king, and then he for fear of Banquo, his old companion, that he should beget kings but be no king himself, he contrived the death of Banquo, and caused him to be murdered on the way as he rode. The next night, being at supper with his noblemen, whom he had bid to a feast, to the which also Banquo should have come, he began to speak of noble Banquo, and to wish that he were there. And as he thus did, standing up to drink a carouse to him, the ghost of Banquo came and sat down in his chair behind him. And he, turning about to sit down again, saw the ghost of Banquo which fronted him so, that he fell into a great passion of fear and fury, uttering many words about his murder, by which, when they heard that Banquo was murdered, they suspected Macbeth. Then

Macduff fled to England to the king's son, and so they raised an army and came into Scotland, and at Dunston Anyse overthrew Macbeth. In the mean time, while Macduff was in England, Macbeth slew Macduff's wife and children, and after, in the battle, Macduff slew Macbeth. Observe also how Macbeth's queen did rise in the night in her sleep, and walked, and talked and confessed all, and the Doctor noted her words.

We can know little for certain about the nature of these Jacobean performances. Presumably the part of Macbeth was played originally by Richard Burbage, who created the title-roles of all the great Shakespeare tragedies. Presumably the parts of Lady Macbeth and Lady Macduff were played by boys; and it is likely that men played the Witches' parts, as they did other crone-roles of the Elizabethan stage.

Presumably the play was costumed in contemporary style; but IV.3.160, where Malcolm seems to recognize Ross as a Scotsman by his clothes, suggests that touches of 'Scottishness' appeared. Certainly the costuming stayed contemporary up to and beyond the time of Garrick, who played the hero in the scarlet coat of an eighteenth-century general. But in 1772 Macklin adopted the tartan and the kilt as more appropriate to the primitive nature of the action; and from that time forward barbaric clothing has prevailed, reaching a climax (one trusts) in the Orson Welles film of 1948 which set the play (evidently) in the sartorial reign of Genghis Khan.

Sir William Davenant refashioned the play, about 1663, into something much more 'regular' or neo-classical; scansion and vocabulary were pruned into line with neo-classical tastes, so that

> *What bloody man is that? He can report,*
> *As seemeth by his plight, of the revolt*
> *The newest state*

becomes

> *What aged man is that? If we may guess*
> *His message by his looks, he can relate*
> *The issue of the battle.*

'Superfluous' or eccentric characters, like the Old Man, the bleeding Captain, and the Porter disappear, or turn into Seyton – here the universal factotum and confidant. I shall discuss later (pages 44–5) the textual problems raised by the *Macbeth* songs in the Davenant version. The point to make here is their appropriateness to a new conception of the play. Davenant introduces a completely new Witch-scene, after Act II, scene 4. On the blasted heath Lady Macduff meets Macduff in flight from Inverness, and the Witches prophesy to them, as earlier to Banquo and Macbeth, and entertain them with a couple of new songs. Davenant's version of *Macbeth* is not only more 'regular' but also more obviously spectacular than Shakespeare's. A contemporary refers to 'The tragedy of *Macbeth*, altered by Sir William Davenant, being dressed in all its finery, as new clothes, new scenes, machines, as flyings for the Witches, with all the singing and dancing in it . . . all excellently performed, being in the nature of an opera.' Presumably it was this version that Pepys saw in 1667, when he referred to *Macbeth* as 'a most excellent play in all respects, especially in divertissement, though it be a deep tragedy; which is a strange perfection in a tragedy, it being most proper here and suitable'. What the discerning Pepys enjoyed, English theatre-goers went on enjoying for more than a century, while the original *Macbeth* vanished. The traditional operatic conception of *Macbeth* continued to hold the stage even after Garrick had (in 1744) deleted most of Davenant's changes. (The same weakening in the sense of supernatural evil is evident in the Verdi *Macbeth* no less than in the Davenant one. Singing witches are likely to be too tuneful to be terrifying, however good the tunes.) The Witches' divertissements continued to be staged into Irving's time: that is, till 1888.

Garrick's *Macbeth* deleted much of Davenant's rewriting, but was by no means a purely Shakespearian text. The most famous Garrick addition was the speech he gave to the dying Macbeth:

> *'Tis done! The scene of life will quickly close.*
> *Ambition's vain delusive dreams are fled,*
> *And now I wake to darkness, guilt and horror.*
> *I cannot bear it! Let me shake it off –*
> *It will not be; my soul is clogged with blood –*
> *I cannot rise! I dare not ask for mercy –*
> *It is too late; hell drags me down; I sink,*
> *I sink – my soul is fled for ever! O – O –*   Dies

The stage-history of *Macbeth* requires, as I have suggested, that we notice the diversion of Shakespeare's play towards external spectacle. When we notice this movement, however, we should also observe that the natural and (as it were) internal spectacle of *Macbeth* was, at the same time, being reduced. The appearance of Banquo's ghost in the banqueting scene (Act III, scene 4) was a famous moment in the Jacobean theatre (as contemporary witness attests). But no one in the scene except Macbeth sees the Ghost; and the rationalizing mind of the eighteenth century was bound to be attracted by the possibility that the Ghost was a figment of Macbeth's imagination. The solitary reader's perception of the inner mind of the hero was assuming precedence over the external and theatrical signs of that mind. The physical presence of one of the race of stage ghosts, with 'their mealy faces, white shirts and red rags stuck on in imitation of blood' was finally dispelled in J. P. Kemble's production of 1794 – a production, be it noted, that introduced new splendours into the Hecat scenes. The learned approved the innovation; but the populace wanted to see the Ghost, and producers were obliged to restore him. Since that time various learned hands have sought to expunge the ghost from this scene, but none has succeeded in affecting the theatrical tradition.

J. P. Kemble's Macbeth was concerned with psychological nuance, as the business of the Ghost may suggest, but we are still, in his reign, in the period of the *noble* Macbeth, projected through a classical mode of acting as slow-moving, dignified, suffering. Kemble's sister, Mrs Siddons, was the most famous of all Lady Macbeths; and it is obvious, from the great wealth of eye-witness accounts, that she contrived to be at once more attractive, more courteous, more forceful, more terrifying than any ordinary human being. The 'statue-like solemnity' of her movements and of her utterance allowed her to convey an impression of the 'giants before the Flood', of grandly primitive simplicity. Later critics, however, complained that she was too overbearing and too scornful of her husband's weakness to provide a truthful image of Shakespeare's Lady – of the wavering and deeply divided nature of one who destroys her own finer self in order to satisfy her husband's ambitions.

The Romantic sense of greatness of spirit as naturally a prey to Childe-Harold-like alternations of extremes – this was better served by the Macbeth of Edmund Kean; for Kean seems to have brought out particularly the terror and dismay that shadow the King's nobility. The movement from noble to ignoble Macbeth was a fairly continuous nineteenth-century movement, and was taken an obvious stage further by Irving at the end of the century. Macbeth, in Irving's interpretation, was obviously unmanned by guilt. A contemporary noted that 'Mr Irving's Macbeth, as he becomes unscrupulous and reckless, becomes also abject.' In the encounter with Banquo's ghost, Macready (in the middle of the nineteenth century) had thrown his cloak over his face ('Hence, horrible shadow') and sunk back into his chair. Irving not only threw his cloak over his face but fell down at the foot of the throne.

Most modern Macbeths are of this breed – anxious, dismayed, hysterical, but lacking in the stature that would terrify us. It is worth noticing that the final duologue of Act III, scene 4, which is the emotional highlight of many modern productions, was hardly mentioned in the accounts of eighteenth-century and nineteenth-century productions.

The obviously primitive setting of *Macbeth*, and the remoteness of its manners from those of modern times, make it a difficult play to modernize. Sir Barry Jackson produced a *Macbeth* in modern dress, in London in 1928, but this was generally disliked. A review noted that 'if conditions and costumes are made modern, criminology must be also'. The Macbeth, who reminded a critic of 'a Scottish gentleman in considerable difficulties', would have been discovered, the same review continued, 'and arrested in a few hours, by the village constable'.

On the other hand the plot of *Macbeth* is clearly strong enough and archetypal enough to survive transposition into quite remote media. The American film *Joe Macbeth* (1955) translated the play into Chicago gang terms. Joe Macbeth, the lieutenant of 'king-pin Duca', the Chicago number one, has future greatness foretold him by Rosie cutting the cards; urged on by his newly wed and ambitious wife, he kills Duca on a lakeshore diving-raft ('the knife knows where to go, Joe. Just follow it'); and later has also to kill Bankie, his former friend. The Chicago inter-gang bloodbath provides a convincing translation of the final scenes of the play.

The Japanese film *Throne of Blood* (1957) makes an even more radical transmutation. Not only is the dialogue in Japanese, but it seems to have little to do with Shake-speare's text. The director's effort has been to externalize Macbeth's mind in terms of visual images rather than words. Hence the importance of the forest, which is here at once an impediment in the way of Washizu's (Macbeth's) conquest of the castle (the kingdom) and a symbol of the natural barbarity of his mind.

Both these adaptations stress the point that, by conquer-ing, Macbeth becomes what Duncan was – the object (rather than the subject) of ambition and treachery. In these terms the plot can be endlessly fertile of imitation.

BACKGROUND OF THE PLAY

Shakespeare found the story of *Macbeth* in two separate sections of Holinshed's *Chronicles* (1587). One section is concerned with the secret murder of King Duff and the other with Macbeth's killing of Duncan (in battle) and his subsequent reign. This was legendary rather than historical material – though something resembling it may well have occurred in the middle of the eleventh century – and Shakespeare (as in the parallel instances of *King Lear* and *Cymbeline*) treated his source with a degree of liberty that was not possible in the Histories. The 'history' of *Macbeth* is, in fact, moral rather than factual history; just as the 'Scotland' of *Macbeth* is a country of the mind rather than a real geographical location. Those who bring to the play experience of the country or the century, beyond what the play provides, are in danger of distorting what is really there. More relevant is the image of Scottish history that appeared on Shakespeare's horizon via the mind of the new King of England – James I.

As noted above, *Macbeth* is generally supposed to have been written in 1606 for performance before James I and his royal guest, King Christian IV of Denmark. The play seems designed to catch at several of James's obsessive interests: first of all at his interest in his native country and its past, and in particular at his pride in his own lineage. The unhistorical figure of Banquo, and the unbroken fertility of the Stuarts, descending directly through nine generations – both of these are made much of in the play, particularly in the dumb-show of Act IV, scene 1, where Stuart monarchs pass before Macbeth's stupefied gaze –

What, will the line stretch out to the crack of doom?

Furthermore, James had written learnedly on witches and was known to have a powerful interest in this subject. In 1605, when he visited Oxford (Shakespeare may have been present), Dr Matthew Gwinn, a Fellow of St John's College, welcomed him with a show of Three Sybils, much approved by James. The three quasi-sybils of Dr Gwinn's show are derived from the 'three women in strange and wild apparel . . . either the Weird Sisters, that is (as ye would say) the goddesses of destiny or else some nymphs or fairies' who accost Macbeth and Banquo in Holinshed's *Chronicles of Scotland*. In Gwinn's entertainment they remind James of the prophecies to Banquo (his supposed ancestor) and then hail the King himself, as (firstly) King of Scotland, (secondly) King of England, and (thirdly) King of Ireland.

In spite of Gwinn's usage, and of Holinshed's descrip-

tion of the ladies as 'goddesses ... nymphs or fairies',
Shakespeare represents *his* Weird Sisters, however, as
traditional Scottish witches, with withered skin, beards,
and a native love of mischief – witches such as had appeared in Forres, and were described by Holinshed as
depriving the monarch of sleep and health, in an episode
that forms part of the primary material of the *Macbeth*
story. Moreover, Shakespeare uses the same witches again
in Act IV, where Holinshed speaks of 'certain wizards, in
whose words he put great confidence', and of 'Witches',
quite distinct from the nymphs or fairies of the earlier
episode. Thus Shakespeare centres the play on a struggle
between the individual and the recurrent forces of demonic
possession, where his source does not.

But the struggle is not simply between an individual
(any individual) and the powers of darkness. The play
offers a continuous study of modes of kingship. Duncan,
Macbeth, Malcolm, and Edward the Confessor reveal com-
plementary insights into the nature of that connexion between Divinity and royal position that James was so
concerned about. Act IV, scene 3, is largely concerned
with definition of 'the king-becoming graces', and its report
of Edward the Confessor's virtues is used to establish the
potency of virtuous kingship in our minds before the play
plunges onward to demonstrate the fate of vicious kingship (and queenship). The episode of Edward's 'touching'
for 'the Evil' (scrofula) seems to have been written, indeed,
to link the play's sense of royal virtue with James. As the
text tells us (IV.3.155):

> *To the succeeding royalty he leaves*
> *The healing benediction.*

By the date of the play James had begun, after some hesita-
tion, to 'touch' for the King's Evil.

We should also notice that the opponents of Divine Kingship are not simply the diabolical forces of evil; they are also traitors and weaklings, equivocators and false believers, such as had been plentifully apparent in the most dramatic antimonarchical episode of James's reign - the Gunpowder Plot of 1605 - and in the subsequent treason trials, especially that of the Provincial of the Jesuit Order in England, Father Garnet. Garnet's trial had excited great detestation because, when he was discovered in lies told to his examiners, he alleged that he had done so in accordance with the doctrine of 'Equivocation', which allowed the faithful to say one thing while holding (but not uttering) mental reservations. This is usually thought to be referred to directly in the Porter's 'Faith, here's an equivocator that could swear in both the scales against either scale, who committed treason enough for God's sake, yet could not equivocate to heaven' (II.3.8–11). Equivocation, the 'double sense' of Macbeth, the swearing and lying that young Macduff refers to in Act IV, scene 2, is indeed a principal mode of the operation of evil forces throughout the play.

Whether the play as we have it in the only surviving authentic text - that of the first Folio (1623) - is the play that was performed at Hampton Court, or the play as seen at The Globe - this has been considered to be another real problem. Simon Forman's account, cited above (pages 30–32), diverges from the play we can read. But should we suppose that there was ever a play corresponding exactly to Forman's account? It seems fairly clear from his wording that he has remembered or consulted Holinshed's chronicle of the reign; which implies uncertainty of memory and contamination from an outside source - both suspicious qualities in a witness. In any case Forman was not writing as a theatrical reporter; he was writing notes on matters that might be useful to remember. Can we blame him, or be surprised, if he did not write down what did not seem worth memorializing?

The shortness of our text (about 2,100 lines) may be thought to point to court origin – James was bored by long performances. On the other hand, the text that reached the printing-house in 1622 (and emerged in the first Folio) is very unlikely to have come from the court, and very likely to have come from the public theatre. The concentration of the action (notice the absence of any sub-plot) is in fact a quality close to the essential life of the play; it is hard to imagine any addition that would not be a dilution. It has sometimes been argued that matters are left unexplained (whether Macbeth had discussed the murder with his wife; whether or not he knew of Cawdor's treachery), but what Shakespeare play does not give rise to such complaints? Nothing essential to *Macbeth* is left in doubt; and the art of chiaroscuro, of leaving the inessential in richly suggestive shadow, is no strange element in Shakespeare's art.

Macbeth is a play of stark disjunctions (murders amid feastings, the laughing Porter at the gate of hell, the whitest innocence beside the blackest treachery, femininity coupled with violence), and the tersest of narrative methods is required. It is hard to imagine that either the Globe *Macbeth* or the court *Macbeth* could have differed in any important respects from the *Macbeth* we have today.

Of course the 'steep tragic contrasts' which I have been describing as essential to the play have often been thought to be the result of corruption rather than design; and it has been assumed, from time to time, that the bleeding Captain, the Old Man of Act II, scene 4, the Porter, young

Macduff, and even the last hundred lines of the play, are non-Shakespearian. These are, however, fairly generally accepted nowadays. The only parts of the play to excite general suspicion today are those involving Hecat, and these deserve fuller discussion.

Hecat appears twice (III.5.1-35, and IV.1.38-43), though she is mentioned on several other occasions, and in both these appearances (as in one other passage, IV.1. 124-31, when she seems to be absent) we have recurrent features different from anything else in the Witch-scenes of *Macbeth*. The poetry of the *Macbeth* Witches is characterized by a four-beat trochaic rhythm:

> *Liver of blaspheming Jew,*
> *Gall of goat, and slips of yew ...*
> *Finger of birth-strangled babe,*
> *Ditch-delivered by a drab,*
> *Make the gruel thick and slab.*

This rhythm is not simply the literary mode that Shakespeare chose, but is rather an essential part of the creation; it is the tone of voice that we must think of as 'natural' to these creatures. It holds, in its drumming insistence, in its obsessively narrow range of effects (hovering between threat and ritual), the key to the quality of their natures. And the rhythm (and so the nature) of Hecat is quite different:

> *And, which is worse, all you have done*
> *Hath been but for a wayward son,*
> *Spiteful and wrathful, who, as others do,*
> *Loves for his own ends, not for you.*

The basic beat here is iambic, and a much greater degree of freedom from steady recurrence seems to be permissible.

The difference that the change from trochaic to iambic metre causes can be seen from a simple rephrasing of the Witches' lines given above. If we had read (with Davenant)

> *The liver of blaspheming Jew,*
> *With gall of goats and slips of yew,*
> *Plucked when the moon was in eclipse,*
> *With a Turk's nose and Tartar's lips;*
> *The finger of a strangled babe*
> *Born of a ditch-delivered drab,*
> *Shall make the gruel thick and slab,*

I suggest that we would have found the passage less terrifying, more 'normal', more acceptable. But not only do the Hecat lines *sound* different; they refer to a different relationship between Macbeth and the Witches. In Act III, scene 5, Hecat rebukes the Witches for unauthorized dealings with Macbeth who

> *Loves for his own ends, not for you.*

The suggestion of *love* between the Witches and any human being is ludicrously unlike anything that we have been led to expect. Moreover the Witches here seem concerned (self-consciously) with entertainment, in a way utterly remote from their characters as earlier established. They dance and sing; and at the end of Act IV, scene 1, they do this specifically to 'cheer up' Macbeth:

FIRST WITCH
>   *But why*
> *Stands Macbeth thus amazedly?*
> *Come, sisters, cheer we up his sprites*
> *And show the best of our delights.*
> *I'll charm the air to give a sound,*
> *While you perform your antic round,*

> *That this great King may kindly say*
> *Our duties did his welcome pay.*
>   Music. The Witches dance; and vanish

MACBETH

> *Where are they? Gone! Let this pernicious hour*
> *Stand aye accursèd in the calendar.*

The discontinuity here between the Witches' efforts and
Macbeth's response seems more than another effect of
contrast. It is as if the two sides were on totally different
wavelengths, or speaking out of different plays.

Mention of the music brings us to the most obvious and
perhaps the most misleading elements in this whole
tangled situation. The two songs named in the Folio text –
'Black spirits etc.' (IV.1.43) and 'Come away, come away
etc.' (III.5.35) – appear (in full) in Sir William Davenant's
rewriting of *Macbeth* for Restoration tastes (*c.* 1663) and
(earlier) in a manuscript play by Thomas Middleton, *The
Witch* – dated between 1609 and 1616. (They are printed in
the explanatory notes to the scenes in question.) The
Middleton play provides the natural setting for these songs,
and there can be little doubt that they were written by
Middleton for his own play. The obvious explanation must
be that they were inserted into *Macbeth* at some point between 1609 and the publication of *Macbeth* in the first
Folio (1623), presumably as part of an expanded version,
used in a revival.

Songs are regular centres of corruption and textual uncertainties in the printed plays of this period. The conditions of their preservation differed in some important ways
from those of the play-texts themselves. They were very
often omitted from the printed texts, and were liable to be
interpolated into plays some time after the first edition.
Presumably, fashions in song-style and in lyric altered

more rapidly than fashions in spoken verse; and the commercial consequence was that theatrical managers required changes here more frequently than in other respects.

We do not have in *Macbeth*, however, the whole texts of the songs that appear in *The Witch*, only the first lines. The reference by catch-lines appears in other plays, it is true, but then the title normally refers to a well-known tune. I believe that *Macbeth* is unique in using catch-lines to refer to songs that are only known from a single dramatic text, and obviously written for that text. It is possible indeed that full texts of the Middleton songs did not appear in any *Macbeth* before the Quarto of 1673 – where they are, presumably, derived from Davenant's version. It is even possible, indeed, that it is the music (probably written by Robert Johnson, musician to the King's Men, in the first decade of the seventeenth century) that is referred to in the Folio *Macbeth*, rather than any particular set of words.

Moreover, even if the full Middleton texts were used in the Jacobean performances of *Macbeth*, it does not follow that the words of Act III, scene 5, or of the two iambic passages in Act IV, scene 1, were also written by Middleton. They are not in the least like the witch-rhetoric of *The Witch*. They exist to introduce the balletic and operatic elements in *Macbeth*, but since songs were regarded as general (and detachable) playhouse property, there is no particular necessity to suppose that Middleton wrote the introductory lines. Their author could well be Shakespeare himself.

FURTHER READING

Among single-volume editions, Kenneth Muir's Arden edition (1951; last revised 1984) remains the most useful. There is an interestingly argued Oxford edition (1990), with elaborate apparatus, edited by Nicholas Brooke; among paperbacks, one should mention the revised Bantam, edited by David Bevington (1988); G. L. Kittredge's edition (1936) is worth consulting for the well-focused fullness of its annotations. The Harrow edition of Watkins and Lemmon (1964) concentrates on the theatrical possibilities of the play, illustrated by line drawings of Globe-type performances. A comprehensive account of scholarship and criticism is to be found in *Macbeth: An Annotated Bibliography* by Thomas Wheeler (The Garland Shakespeare Biographies, 1990).

SOURCES

The relevant passages from Holinshed's *Chronicle*, the principal source, are printed in Furness's New Variorum edition (1873), in Kenneth Muir's and in Nicholas Brooke's. Geoffrey Bullough's *Narrative and Dramatic Sources of Shakespeare*, Volume VII (1973), discusses and prints all known sources and analogues.

THE PLAY

(1) *Classic Criticism*

Brian Vickers' *Shakespeare: The Cultural Heritage*, six volumes (1974–81), presents substantial extracts from theatrical and literary comments up to 1801. The most famous literary essay on *Macbeth* – De Quincey's 'On the Knocking on the Gate in *Macbeth*' – is available (slightly abbreviated) in Furness. R. G. Moulton's *Shakespeare as a Dramatic Artist* (1885) remains the most pertinently accessible of Victorian treatments. Moulton's 'arrangement' of *Macbeth* as a Greek tragedy (in *The Ancient Classical Drama*, 1890) is a stimulating exercise in comparative criticism. Scholarship that opens up the background of the play can be sampled in Walter Clyde Curry's essay on 'Demonic Metaphysics' in his *Shakespeare's Philosophical Patterns* (1937), in Willard Farnham's *Shakespeare's Tragic Frontier* (1950) and in H. N. Paul, *The Royal Play of Macbeth* (1950) – but see the comments on Paul in Muir's Appendix D and in the Appendix to Chapter 8 in J. R. Brown's *Focus on 'Macbeth'* (1981). A. C. Bradley's chapter in *Shakespearean Tragedy* (1904) remains unsurpassed in its accurate attention to detail coupled with a coherent and lucid theoretical basis. But, in so far as this coherence depends on a subordination of the poetry spoken to the person speaking, it has excited rejection, first in L. C. Knights' 1933 essay 'How Many Children Had Lady Macbeth?' – reprinted in *Explorations* (1946) – and subsequently in many works concerned to validate the images in the play as the source of its inner meaning, as in Cleanth Brooks' 'The Naked Babe and the Cloak of Manliness' in *The Well-Wrought Urn* (1942) and in G. Wilson Knight's *The Wheel of Fire* (1930) and *The Imperial Theme* (1931). E. M. W. Tillyard pointed out *Macbeth*'s relation to the History Plays in his *Shakespeare's History Plays* (1944).

(2) *Modernist Criticism*

Judged by the size of the bibliography, *Macbeth* seems in the last three decades to have attracted less critical interest than the other 'Bradleian' tragedies – *Othello*, *King Lear* and *Hamlet*. The classical simplicity of the plot, what Emrys Jones (*Scenic Form in Shakespeare*, 1971) has called the 'elegance' and 'formal coherence' of its plotting and the apparent determinism of its moral structure, with good and evil placed at opposite poles, may have discouraged further essays in description. Modernist criticism has chosen to go behind the apparently tidy coherence that classic criticism described, concentrating, like the New Critics of the thirties, on the disruptive energy that emerges in the poetry of the play. But the modernists are less interested in describing this as part of a moral pattern than as an indicator of the suppressed energies of political groups opposed to the Stuart kings. Feminism and radical politics (not always separable) have provided the principal vocabularies for this enterprise.

The feminist mode finds an obvious justification in the play's recurrent interest in 'manliness' (violent soldiership) and in its exploration of the consequences of this in the contrasting fates of husband and wife. Freud had given his blessing to this enquiry in a brief discussion on the effect of 'success' in fragmenting character (a point taken up again in Barbara Everett's *Young Hamlet* (1989)). Freud is particularly concerned with the incoherence of the victim-wife, Lady Macbeth (see *The Standard Edition of the Complete Works*, Vol 4 (1957), pp. 318–24). Janet Adelman – in *Cannibals, Witches and Divorce*, ed. Marjorie Garber (1987) – replaces Bradley's moral universals with Freud's psychological ones and sees Macbeth's career as a history of psychic disorientation, requiring him to take refuge in the fantasy of total maleness in order to cope with female domination (appearing in both the Witches and Lady Macbeth).

The disruption of 'conformist' views produced by reading the play from the point of view of gender politics can also be achieved in more purely historical terms. The recentness of the Gunpowder Plot of 1605 and the trials of Jesuit 'traitors' (referred to in the Porter's speech) have suggested to some that the play has a hidden political agenda. See Stephen

Mullaney's article in *ELH* 47 (1980), 32–47. David Norbrook's essay on *Macbeth*, printed in Sharpe and Zwicker, *Politics of Discourse* (1987), argues against the classic position that the play turns on an absolute contrast between the tyrant Macbeth and the good king Duncan. He finds in the background of the play and in Scottish history (drawing on Arthur M. Clark's *Murder under Trust*, 1981) evidence of anti-monarchical currents of thought and deduces Shakespeare's imaginative sympathy with such thoughts. Alan Sinfield in *Faultlines* (1992) offers a very similar view (Duncan is delegitimized by the violence needed to sustain him; in a world sustained by violence Macbeth has no other way of expressing political opposition.) Compare also the essay by Michael Hawkins in John R. Brown's *Focus on Macbeth* (1981).

Brown's collection concentrates mainly on what may be called 'the psychology of performance'. Sinfield's more recent collection of essays (1992) focuses on modernist positions. *Shakespeare Survey 19* (1966) is devoted to *Macbeth* and contains a survey of critical studies; many of the essays in the volume are reprinted in *Aspects of 'Macbeth'*, edited by Kenneth Muir and Philip Edwards (1977). R. A. Foakes has an excellent bibliographical essay in Stanley Wells's *Shakespeare: A Bibliographical Guide* (1990).

STAGE HISTORY

Stage history has occupied more space than usual in recent writings on *Macbeth*, perhaps because theatre allows more scope for a free play of interpretation. Stage history is discussed in the New Cambridge edition by J. Dover Wilson (1947), in Brooke's Oxford edition and in A. C. Sprague's *Shakespeare and the Actors* (1944). Dennis Bartholomeusz's *Macbeth and the Players* (1969) gives an illuminating account of stage actions from 1610 to 1964. Marvin Rosenberg, *The Masks of Macbeth* (1978), takes the reader through the play and at each point describes various theatrical realizations. Gordon Williams, in *Macbeth: Text and Performance* (1985), offers a useful set of summary points. The Cornmarket Press has issued facsimiles of playhouse texts for 1671, 1673, 1674, 1753, 1761 and 1794. The manuscript of Middleton's *The Witch* is printed as a Malone Society Reprint (eds. Greg and Wilson, 1948–50). The Witch-scenes from *The Witch* are printed in Furness. Davenant's operatic version (written before 1668, published in 1674) appears in Furness, in Christopher Spencer's *Five Restoration Adaptations of Shakespeare* (1965) and in a full scholarly edition by the same author in 1961. The Orson Welles and Polanski films, the BBC Shakespeare Series production and the Royal Shakespeare Theatre version with Ian McKellen and Judi Dench are available in video cassette.

THE CHARACTERS IN THE PLAY

DUNCAN, King of Scotland
MALCOLM ⎫
DONALBAIN ⎭ his sons
MACBETH, Thane of Glamis, later of Cawdor, later
  King of Scotland
BANQUO ⎫
MACDUFF ⎪
LENNOX ⎪
ROSS ⎬ Thanes of Scotland
MENTETH ⎪
ANGUS ⎪
CATHNESS ⎭

FLEANCE, Banquo's son
SEYWARD, Earl of Northumberland
YOUNG SEYWARD, his son
SEYTON, Macbeth's armour-bearer
SON OF MACDUFF
A Captain
An English Doctor
A Scottish Doctor
A Porter
An Old Man

LADY MACBETH
WIFE OF MACDUFF
Gentlewoman attendant on Lady Macbeth
Three Weird Sisters
Three other Witches

THE CHARACTERS IN THE PLAY

HECAT
Apparitions

Three Murderers
Other Murderers

Lords, Gentlemen, Officers, Soldiers
Attendants, Messengers

Thunder and lightning. Enter three Witches

FIRST WITCH

When shall we three meet again?
In thunder, lightning, or in rain?

SECOND WITCH

When the hurly-burly's done,
When the battle's lost and won.

THIRD WITCH

That will be ere the set of sun.

FIRST WITCH

Where the place?

SECOND WITCH   Upon the heath.

THIRD WITCH

There to meet with Macbeth.

FIRST WITCH

I come, Grey-Malkin.

SECOND WITCH   Padock calls!

THIRD WITCH   Anon!

ALL

Fair is foul, and foul is fair.
Hover through the fog and filthy air.   *Exeunt* 10

Alarum within I.2
Enter King Duncan, Malcolm, Donalbain, Lennox,
with Attendants, meeting a bleeding Captain

KING

What bloody man is that? He can report,

    As seemeth by his plight, of the revolt
    The newest state.

MALCOLM   This is the sergeant
    Who like a good and hardy soldier fought
    'Gainst my captivity. Hail, brave friend!
    Say to the King the knowledge of the broil
    As thou didst leave it.

CAPTAIN   Doubtful it stood,
    As two spent swimmers that do cling together
    And choke their art. The merciless Macdonwald –
10   Worthy to be a rebel, for to that
    The multiplying villainies of nature
    Do swarm upon him – from the Western Isles
    Of kerns and galloglasses is supplied,
    And fortune on his damnèd quarrel smiling
    Showed like a rebel's whore. But all's too weak:
    For brave Macbeth – well he deserves that name –
    Disdaining fortune, with his brandished steel,
    Which smoked with bloody execution,
    Like valour's minion carvèd out his passage
20   Till he faced the slave –
    Which ne'er shook hands nor bade farewell to him
    Till he unseamed him from the nave to the chops,
    And fixed his head upon our battlements.

KING
    O valiant cousin! Worthy gentleman!

CAPTAIN
    As, whence the sun 'gins his reflection,
    Shipwracking storms and direful thunders;
    So, from that spring whence comfort seemed to come,
    Discomfort swells. Mark, King of Scotland, mark!
    No sooner justice had, with valour armed,
30   Compelled these skipping kerns to trust their heels
    But the Norweyan lord, surveying vantage,

With furbished arms and new supplies of men,
Began a fresh assault.

KING   Dismayed not this
Our captains, Macbeth and Banquo?

CAPTAIN   Yes –
As sparrows, eagles, or the hare, the lion.
If I say sooth I must report they were
As cannons overcharged with double cracks;
So they
Doubly redoubled strokes upon the foe.
Except they meant to bathe in reeking wounds   40
Or memorize another Golgotha
I cannot tell.
– But I am faint; my gashes cry for help.

KING
So well thy words become thee as thy wounds,
They smack of honour both. Go get him surgeons.

Exit Captain with Attendants

Enter Ross and Angus

Who comes here?

MALCOLM   The worthy Thane of Ross.

LENNOX
What a haste looks through his eyes!
So should he look that seems to speak things strange.

ROSS
God save the King!

KING
Whence cam'st thou, worthy thane?

ROSS   From Fife, great King,   50
Where the Norweyan banners flout the sky
And fan our people cold.
Norway himself, with terrible numbers,
Assisted by that most disloyal traitor,
The Thane of Cawdor, began a dismal conflict,

55

Till that Bellona's bridegroom, lapped in proof,
Confronted him with self-comparisons,
Point against point-rebellious, arm 'gainst arm,
Curbing his lavish spirit; and to conclude,
The victory fell on us –

60 KING   Great happiness!

ROSS

– That now Sweno, the Norways' king,
Craves composition;
Nor would we deign him burial of his men
Till he disbursèd at Saint Colm's Inch
Ten thousand dollars to our general use.

KING

No more that Thane of Cawdor shall deceive
Our bosom interest. Go pronounce his present death,
And with his former title greet Macbeth.

ROSS

I'll see it done.

KING

70 What he hath lost, noble Macbeth hath won.   *Exeunt*

I.3   *Thunder. Enter the three Witches*

FIRST WITCH Where hast thou been, sister?
SECOND WITCH Killing swine.
THIRD WITCH Sister, where thou?
FIRST WITCH

A sailor's wife had chestnuts in her lap,
And munched and munched and munched. 'Give me,'
          quoth I.
'Aroint thee, witch!' the rump-fed ronyon cries.
Her husband's to Aleppo gone, master o'the *Tiger*.
          But in a sieve I'll thither sail
          And like a rat without a tail

56

I'll do, I'll do, and I'll do.   10

SECOND WITCH
 I'll give thee a wind.

FIRST WITCH
 Th'art kind.

THIRD WITCH
 And I another.

FIRST WITCH
 I myself have all the other.
 And the very ports they blow
 All the quarters that they know
 I'the shipman's card.
 I'll drain him dry as hay;
 Sleep shall neither night nor day
 Hang upon his penthouse lid.   20
 He shall live a man forbid.
 Weary sev'n-nights nine times nine
 Shall he dwindle, peak, and pine.
 Though his bark cannot be lost,
 Yet it shall be tempest-tossed.
 Look what I have!

SECOND WITCH   Show me, show me!

FIRST WITCH
 Here I have a pilot's thumb,
 Wracked as homeward he did come.

Drum within.

THIRD WITCH
 A drum! a drum!
 Macbeth doth come.   30

ALL
 The Weird Sisters, hand in hand,
 Posters of the sea and land,
 Thus do go, about, about;
 Thrice to thine, and thrice to mine,
 And thrice again, to make up nine.

Peace! The charm's wound up.

Enter Macbeth and Banquo

MACBETH

So foul and fair a day I have not seen.

BANQUO

How far is't called to Forres? What are these,
So withered and so wild in their attire,
40 That look not like the inhabitants o'the earth,
And yet are on't? Live you? Or are you aught
That man may question? You seem to understand me
By each at once her choppy finger laying
Upon her skinny lips. You should be women;
And yet your beards forbid me to interpret
That you are so.

MACBETH   Speak if you can! What are you?

FIRST WITCH

All hail, Macbeth! Hail to thee, Thane of Glamis!

SECOND WITCH

All hail, Macbeth! Hail to thee, Thane of Cawdor!

THIRD WITCH

All hail, Macbeth, that shalt be king hereafter!

BANQUO

50 Good sir, why do you start, and seem to fear
Things that do sound so fair? – I'the name of truth,
Are ye fantastical, or that indeed
Which outwardly ye show? My noble partner
You greet with present grace, and great prediction
Of noble having and of royal hope
That he seems rapt withal. To me you speak not.
If you can look into the seeds of time
And say which grain will grow and which will not,
Speak then to me who neither beg nor fear
60 Your favours nor your hate.

FIRST WITCH
  Hail!
SECOND WITCH
  Hail!
THIRD WITCH
  Hail!
FIRST WITCH
  Lesser than Macbeth, and greater.
SECOND WITCH
  Not so happy, yet much happier.
THIRD WITCH
  Thou shalt get kings, though thou be none.
  So all hail, Macbeth and Banquo!
FIRST WITCH
  Banquo and Macbeth, all hail!
MACBETH
  Stay, you imperfect speakers! Tell me more!
  By Sinell's death I know I am Thane of Glamis;   70
  But how of Cawdor? The Thane of Cawdor lives
  A prosperous gentleman. And to be king
  Stands not within the prospect of belief –
  No more than to be Cawdor. Say from whence
  You owe this strange intelligence; or why
  Upon this blasted heath you stop our way
  With such prophetic greeting? Speak, I charge you!
                                        Witches vanish

BANQUO
  The earth hath bubbles as the water has,
  And these are of them. Whither are they vanished?
MACBETH
  Into the air; and what seemed corporal   80
  Melted, as breath into the wind. Would they had stayed!
BANQUO
  Were such things here as we do speak about?

Or have we eaten on the insane root
That takes the reason prisoner?

MACBETH

Your children shall be kings.

BANQUO   You shall be king.

MACBETH

And Thane of Cawdor too, went it not so?

BANQUO

To the selfsame tune and words. Who's here?
    Enter Ross and Angus

ROSS

The King hath happily received, Macbeth,
The news of thy success; and when he reads
90 Thy personal venture in the rebels' fight
His wonders and his praises do contend
Which should be thine, or his. Silenced with that,
In viewing o'er the rest o'the selfsame day
He finds thee in the stout Norweyan ranks,
Nothing afeard of what thyself didst make,
Strange images of death. As thick as hail
Came post with post; and every one did bear
Thy praises, in his kingdom's great defence,
And poured them down before him.

ANGUS   We are sent
100 To give thee from our royal master thanks;
Only to herald thee into his sight,
Not pay thee.

ROSS

And, for an earnest of a greater honour,
He bade me from him call thee Thane of Cawdor
In which addition, hail, most worthy thane,
For it is thine.

BANQUO   What! Can the devil speak true?

MACBETH

The Thane of Cawdor lives. Why do you dress me

In borrowed robes?

ANGUS   Who was the Thane lives yet;
But under heavy judgement bears that life
Which he deserves to lose. Whether he was combined   110
With those of Norway, or did line the rebel
With hidden help and vantage, or that with both
He laboured in his country's wrack, I know not;
But treasons capital, confessed, and proved
Have overthrown him.

MACBETH (*aside*)   Glamis, and Thane of Cawdor!
The greatest is behind. – Thanks for your pains.
(*to Banquo*) Do you not hope your children shall be
         kings,
When those that gave the Thane of Cawdor to me
Promised no less to them?

BANQUO   That trusted home
Might yet enkindle you unto the crown   120
Besides the Thane of Cawdor. But 'tis strange;
And oftentimes, to win us to our harm,
The instruments of darkness tell us truths;
Win us with honest trifles, to betray's
In deepest consequence.
Cousins, a word, I pray you.
      They walk apart

MACBETH (*aside*)   Two truths are told
As happy prologues to the swelling Act
Of the imperial theme. – I thank you, gentlemen.
(*aside*) This supernatural soliciting
Cannot be ill, cannot be good. If ill,   130
Why hath it given me earnest of success
Commencing in a truth? I am Thane of Cawdor.
If good, why do I yield to that suggestion
Whose horrid image doth unfix my hair,
And make my seated heart knock at my ribs
Against the use of nature? Present fears

Are less than horrible imaginings.
My thought, whose murder yet is but fantastical,
Shakes so my single state of man
140   That function is smothered in surmise,
And nothing is but what is not.

BANQUO Look how our partner's rapt.

MACBETH (*aside*)
If chance will have me king, why chance may crown me
Without my stir.

BANQUO   New honours come upon him
Like our strange garments, cleave not to their mould
But with the aid of use.

MACBETH (*aside*)   Come what come may,
Time and the hour runs through the roughest day.

BANQUO
Worthy Macbeth, we stay upon your leisure.

MACBETH
Give me your favour. My dull brain was wrought
150   With things forgotten. Kind gentlemen, your pains
Are registered where every day I turn
The leaf to read them. Let us toward the King.
(*to Banquo*) Think upon what hath chanced, and at more
          time,
The interim having weighed it, let us speak
Our free hearts each to other.

BANQUO   Very gladly.

MACBETH
Till then, enough! – Come, friends.   *Exeunt*

KING

Is execution done on Cawdor?
Are not those in commission yet returned?

MALCOLM

My liege,
They are not yet come back. But I have spoke
With one that saw him die, who did report
That very frankly he confessed his treasons,
Implored your highness' pardon, and set forth
A deep repentance. Nothing in his life
Became him like the leaving it. He died
As one that had been studied in his death   10
To throw away the dearest thing he owed
As 'twere a careless trifle.

KING   There's no art
To find the mind's construction in the face.
He was a gentleman on whom I built
An absolute trust.

Enter Macbeth, Banquo, Ross, and Angus
                    O worthiest cousin!
The sin of my ingratitude even now
Was heavy on me. Thou art so far before,
That swiftest wing of recompense is slow
To overtake thee. Would thou hadst less deserved,
That the proportion both of thanks and payment   20
Might have been mine. Only I have left to say,
'More is thy due than more than all can pay.'

MACBETH

The service and the loyalty I owe,
In doing it, pays itself. Your highness' part
Is to receive our duties; and our duties
Are to your throne and state, children and servants,

Which do but what they should by doing everything
Safe toward your love and honour.

KING   Welcome hither.
I have begun to plant thee, and will labour
To make thee full of growing. – Noble Banquo,
That hast no less deserved, nor must be known
No less to have done so, let me enfold thee
And hold thee to my heart.

BANQUO   There if I grow,
The harvest is your own.

KING   My plenteous joys,
Wanton in fulness, seek to hide themselves
In drops of sorrow. Sons, kinsmen, thanes,
And you whose places are the nearest, know
We will establish our estate upon
Our eldest, Malcolm, whom we name hereafter
The Prince of Cumberland: which honour must
Not unaccompanied invest him only,
But signs of nobleness, like stars, shall shine
On all deservers. From hence to Inverness,
And bind us further to you.

MACBETH
The rest is labour, which is not used for you.
I'll be myself the harbinger and make joyful
The hearing of my wife with your approach;
So humbly take my leave.

KING   My worthy Cawdor!

MACBETH (aside)
The Prince of Cumberland! That is a step
On which I must fall down, or else o'erleap,
For in my way it lies. Stars, hide your fires,
Let not light see my black and deep desires.
The eye wink at the hand; yet let that be
Which the eye fears, when it is done, to see.   Exit

KING

    True, worthy Banquo; he is full so valiant,
And in his commendations I am fed;
It is a banquet to me. Let's after him
Whose care is gone before to bid us welcome.
It is a peerless kinsman.   *Flourish. Exeunt*

    Enter Macbeth's Wife alone with a letter   I.5

LADY *They met me in the day of success, and I have learned*
by the perfectest report they have more in them than mortal
knowledge. When I burned in desire to question them fur-
ther, they made themselves air, into which they vanished.
Whiles I stood rapt in the wonder of it, came missives from
the King, who all-hailed me Thane of Cawdor; by which
title before these Weird Sisters saluted me, and referred me
to the coming on of time with, 'Hail, king that shalt be.'
This have I thought good to deliver thee, my dearest partner
of greatness, that thou mightest not lose the dues of re- 10
joicing by being ignorant of what greatness is promised thee.
Lay it to thy heart, and farewell.
Glamis thou art, and Cawdor, and shalt be
What thou art promised. Yet do I fear thy nature:
It is too full o'the milk of human-kindness
To catch the nearest way. Thou wouldst be great,
Art not without ambition, but without
The illness should attend it. What thou wouldst highly
That wouldst thou holily, wouldst not play false,
And yet wouldst wrongly win. Thou'dst have, great
      Glamis,
                           20
That which cries, 'Thus thou must do' if thou have it,
And that which rather thou dost fear to do
Than wishest should be undone. Hie thee hither
That I may pour my spirits in thine ear,

65

And chastise with the valour of my tongue
All that impedes thee from the golden round
Which fate and metaphysical aid doth seem
To have thee crowned withal.

    Enter Messenger   What is your tidings?

MESSENGER

The King comes here tonight.

LADY   Thou'rt mad to say it!

30 Is not thy master with him? Who, were't so,
Would have informed for preparation.

MESSENGER

So please you, it is true. Our Thane is coming;
One of my fellows had the speed of him,
Who, almost dead for breath, had scarcely more
Than would make up his message.

LADY   Give him tending:
He brings great news.   *Exit Messenger*
                The raven himself is hoarse
That croaks the fatal entrance of Duncan
Under my battlements. Come, you spirits
That tend on mortal thoughts, unsex me here
40 And fill me from the crown to the toe top-full
Of direst cruelty. Make thick my blood;
Stop up the access and passage to remorse,
That no compunctious visitings of nature
Shake my fell purpose, nor keep peace between
The effect and it. Come to my woman's breasts
And take my milk for gall, you murdering ministers,
Wherever, in your sightless substances,
You wait on nature's mischief. Come, thick night,
And pall thee in the dunnest smoke of hell,
50 That my keen knife see not the wound it makes,
Nor heaven peep through the blanket of the dark
To cry, 'Hold, hold!'

Enter Macbeth

                    Great Glamis, worthy Cawdor!
Greater than both by the all-hail hereafter!
Thy letters have transported me beyond
This ignorant present, and I feel now
The future in the instant.

MACBETH   My dearest love,
Duncan comes here tonight.

LADY   And when goes hence?

MACBETH

Tomorrow, as he purposes.

LADY   O never
Shall sun that morrow see!
Your face, my thane, is as a book where men   60
May read strange matters. To beguile the time
Look like the time, bear welcome in your eye,
Your hand, your tongue; look like the innocent flower,
But be the serpent under't. He that's coming
Must be provided for; and you shall put
This night's great business into my dispatch,
Which shall to all our nights and days to come
Give solely sovereign sway and masterdom.

MACBETH

We will speak further.

LADY   Only look up clear:
To alter favour ever is to fear.   70
Leave all the rest to me.   *Exeunt*

Hautboys and torches. Enter King Duncan, Malcolm, I.6
Donalbain. Banquo, Lennox, Macduff, Ross, Angus,
and Attendants

KING

This castle hath a pleasant seat; the air

Nimbly and sweetly recommends itself
Unto our gentle senses.

BANQUO   This guest of summer,
The temple-haunting martlet, does approve
By his loved mansionry that the heaven's breath
Smells wooingly here; no jutty, frieze,
Buttress, nor coign of vantage, but this bird
Hath made his pendent bed and procreant cradle;
Where they most breed and haunt I have observed
The air is delicate.

Enter Lady Macbeth

10 KING   See, see, our honoured hostess –
The love that follows us sometime is our trouble,
Which still we thank as love. Herein I teach you
How you shall bid 'God 'ield us' for your pains,
And thank us for your trouble.

LADY   All our service
In every point twice done and then done double
Were poor and single business to contend
Against those honours deep and broad wherewith
Your majesty loads our house. For those of old,
And the late dignities heaped up to them,
We rest your hermits.

20 KING   Where's the Thane of Cawdor?
We coursed him at the heels and had a purpose
To be his purveyor; but he rides well,
And his great love, sharp as his spur, hath holp him
To his home before us. Fair and noble hostess,
We are your guest tonight.

LADY   Your servants ever
Have theirs, themselves, and what is theirs, in compt,
To make their audit at your highness' pleasure,
Still to return your own.

KING   Give me your hand;

Conduct me to mine host. We love him highly,
And shall continue our graces towards him.   30
By your leave, hostess.   *He kisses her. Exeunt*

Hautboys. Torches. Enter a Sewer and divers Servants I.7
with dishes and service over the stage. Then enter
Macbeth

MACBETH
If it were done when 'tis done, then 'twere well
It were done quickly. If the assassination
Could trammel up the consequence, and catch
With his surcease success - that but this blow
Might be the be-all and the end-all! - here,
But here, upon this bank and shoal of time,
We'd jump the life to come. But in these cases
We still have judgement here - that we but teach
Bloody instructions, which, being taught, return
To plague the inventor. This even-handed justice   10
Commends the ingredience of our poisoned chalice
To our own lips. He's here in double trust:
First, as I am his kinsman and his subject,
Strong both against the deed; then, as his host,
Who should against his murderer shut the door,
Not bear the knife myself. Besides, this Duncan
Hath borne his faculties so meek, hath been
So clear in his great office, that his virtues
Will plead like angels, trumpet-tongued against
The deep damnation of his taking-off;   20
And Pity, like a naked new-born babe
Striding the blast, or heaven's cherubin, horsed
Upon the sightless curriers of the air,
Shall blow the horrid deed in every eye,
That tears shall drown the wind. I have no spur

69

To prick the sides of my intent but only
Vaulting ambition which o'erleaps itself
And falls on the other.

Enter Lady Macbeth

How now? What news?

LADY

He has almost supped. Why have you left the chamber?

MACBETH

Hath he asked for me?

30 LADY   Know you not he has?

MACBETH

We will proceed no further in this business.
He hath honoured me of late, and I have bought
Golden opinions from all sorts of people
Which would be worn now in their newest gloss,
Not cast aside so soon.

LADY   Was the hope drunk
Wherein you dressed yourself? Hath it slept since?
And wakes it now to look so green and pale
At what it did so freely? From this time
Such I account thy love. Art thou afeard

40 To be the same in thine own act and valour
As thou art in desire? Wouldst thou have that
Which thou esteem'st the ornament of life,
And live a coward in thine own esteem,
Letting 'I dare not' wait upon 'I would',
Like the poor cat i'the adage?

MACBETH   Prithee peace.
I dare do all that may become a man;
Who dares do more is none.

LADY   What beast was't then
That made you break this enterprise to me?
When you durst do it, then you were a man;

50 And to be more than what you were, you would

Be so much more the man. Nor time nor place
Did then adhere, and yet you would make both.
They have made themselves, and that their fitness now
Does unmake you. I have given suck, and know
How tender 'tis to love the babe that milks me;
I would while it was smiling in my face
Have plucked my nipple from his boneless gums
And dashed the brains out, had I so sworn as you
Have done to this.

MACBETH   If we should fail?

LADY   We fail!
But screw your courage to the sticking place,   60
And we'll not fail. When Duncan is asleep –
Whereto the rather shall his day's hard journey
Soundly invite him - his two chamberlains
Will I with wine and wassail so convince
That memory, the warder of the brain,
Shall be a-fume, and the receipt of reason
A limbeck only. When in swinish sleep
Their drenchèd natures lies as in a death,
What cannot you and I perform upon
The unguarded Duncan? What not put upon   70
His spongy officers, who shall bear the guilt
Of our great quell?

MACBETH   Bring forth men-children only!
For thy undaunted mettle should compose
Nothing but males. Will it not be received,
When we have marked with blood those sleepy two
Of his own chamber, and used their very daggers,
That they have done't?

LADY   Who dares receive it other,
As we shall make our griefs and clamour roar
Upon his death?

MACBETH   I am settled; and bend up

80 Each corporal agent to this terrible feat.
Away, and mock the time with fairest show:
False face must hide what the false heart doth know.

Exeunt

*

II.1 *Enter Banquo, and Fleance with a torch before him*

BANQUO

How goes the night, boy?

FLEANCE

The moon is down; I have not heard the clock.

BANQUO

And she goes down at twelve.

FLEANCE   I take't 'tis later, sir.

BANQUO

Hold, take my sword. There's husbandry in heaven:
Their candles are all out. Take thee that too.
A heavy summons lies like lead upon me
And yet I would not sleep. Merciful powers,
Restrain in me the cursèd thoughts that nature
Gives way to in repose.

Enter Macbeth and a Servant with a torch
                                Give me my sword!

10 Who's there?

MACBETH

A friend.

BANQUO

What, sir, not yet at rest? The King's a-bed.
He hath been in unusual pleasure,
And sent forth great largess to your offices.
This diamond he greets your wife withal
By the name of most kind hostess, and shut up
In measureless content.

MACBETH   Being unprepared
  Our will became the servant to defect,
  Which else should free have wrought.
BANQUO   All's well.
  I dreamt last night of the three Weird Sisters.   20
  To you they have showed some truth.
MACBETH   I think not of them.
  Yet, when we can entreat an hour to serve,
  We would spend it in some words upon that business,
  If you would grant the time.
BANQUO   At your kind'st leisure.
MACBETH
  If you shall cleave to my consent when 'tis,
  It shall make honour for you.
BANQUO   So I lose none
  In seeking to augment it, but still keep
  My bosom franchised and allegiance clear,
  I shall be counselled.
MACBETH   Good repose the while.
BANQUO
  Thanks, sir; the like to you.   *Exit Banquo and Fleance* 30
MACBETH
  Go bid thy mistress, when my drink is ready
  She strike upon the bell. Get thee to bed.

                                         Exit Servant

  Is this a dagger which I see before me,
  The handle toward my hand? Come, let me clutch thee –
  I have thee not and yet I see thee still!
  Art thou not, fatal vision, sensible
  To feeling as to sight? Or art thou but
  A dagger of the mind, a false creation,
  Proceeding from the heat-oppressèd brain?
  I see thee yet, in form as palpable   40
  As this which now I draw.

73

Thou marshall'st me the way that I was going,
And such an instrument I was to use. –
Mine eyes are made the fools o'the other senses,
Or else worth all the rest. – I see thee still;
And, on thy blade and dudgeon, gouts of blood,
Which was not so before. There's no such thing.
It is the bloody business which informs
Thus to mine eyes. Now o'er the one half-world
50 Nature seems dead, and wicked dreams abuse
The curtained sleep. Witchcraft celebrates
Pale Hecat's offerings; and withered Murder,
Alarumed by his sentinel the wolf,
Whose howl's his watch, thus with his stealthy pace,
With Tarquin's ravishing strides, towards his design
Moves like a ghost. Thou sure and firm-set earth,
Hear not my steps, which way they walk, for fear
Thy very stones prate of my whereabout
And take the present horror from the time
60 Which now suits with it. – Whiles I threat, he lives:
Words to the heat of deeds too cold breath gives.
    A bell rings
I go, and it is done; the bell invites me.
Hear it not, Duncan, for it is a knell
That summons thee to heaven or to hell.   *Exit*

II.2   *Enter Lady Macbeth*

LADY

That which hath made them drunk hath made me bold;
What hath quenched them hath given me fire. – Hark! –
    Peace!
It was the owl that shrieked, the fatal bellman
Which gives the stern'st good-night. He is about it.
The doors are open, and the surfeited grooms

Do mock their charge with snores; I have drugged their
    possets
That death and nature do contend about them
Whether they live or die.

MACBETH (*within*)   Who's there? What, ho!

LADY
Alack, I am afraid they have awaked,
And 'tis not done. The attempt and not the deed   10
Confounds us. - Hark! - I laid their daggers ready;
He could not miss 'em. Had he not resembled
My father as he slept, I had done't.

    Enter Macbeth, carrying two bloodstained daggers
                          My husband!

MACBETH
I have done the deed. Didst thou not hear a noise?

LADY
I heard the owl-scream and the cricket's cry.
Did not you speak?

MACBETH   When?

LADY   Now.

MACBETH   As I descended?

LADY
Ay.

MACBETH
Hark!
Who lies i'the second chamber?

LADY   Donalbain.

MACBETH (*looks at his hands*)
This is a sorry sight.   20

LADY
A foolish thought, to say a sorry sight.

MACBETH
There's one did laugh in's sleep, and one cried 'Murder!'
That they did wake each other. I stood and heard them.

But they did say their prayers and addressed them
Again to sleep.

LADY   There are two lodged together.

MACBETH

One cried 'God bless us' and 'Amen' the other,
As they had seen me with these hangman's hands.
Listening their fear I could not say 'Amen'
When they did say 'God bless us.'

LADY

30 Consider it not so deeply.

MACBETH

But wherefore could not I pronounce 'Amen'?
I had most need of blessing, and 'Amen'
Stuck in my throat.

LADY   These deeds must not be thought
After these ways; so, it will make us mad.

MACBETH

Methought I heard a voice cry, 'Sleep no more!
Macbeth does murder sleep – the innocent sleep,
Sleep that knits up the ravelled sleave of care,
The death of each day's life, sore labour's bath,
Balm of hurt minds, great nature's second course,
Chief nourisher in life's feast.'

40 LADY   What do you mean?

MACBETH

Still it cried 'Sleep no more' to all the house;
'Glamis hath murdered sleep, and therefore Cawdor
Shall sleep no more, Macbeth shall sleep no more.'

LADY

Who was it that thus cried? Why, worthy thane,
You do unbend your noble strength, to think
So brain-sickly of things. Go, get some water,
And wash this filthy witness from your hand.
Why did you bring these daggers from the place?

They must lie there. Go, carry them and smear
The sleepy grooms with blood.

MACBETH   I'll go no more.   50
I am afraid to think what I have done;
Look on't again I dare not.

LADY   Infirm of purpose!
Give me the daggers. The sleeping and the dead
Are but as pictures. 'Tis the eye of childhood
That fears a painted devil. If he do bleed,
I'll gild the faces of the grooms withal,
For it must seem their guilt.   *Exit*
        Knock within

MACBETH   Whence is that knocking?
How is't with me when every noise appals me?
What hands are here! Ha – they pluck out mine eyes!
Will all great Neptune's ocean wash this blood   60
Clean from my hand? No, this my hand will rather
The multitudinous seas incarnadine,
Making the green one red.
        Enter Lady Macbeth

LADY
My hands are of your colour; but I shame
To wear a heart so white.
        Knock

                              I hear a knocking
At the south entry. Retire we to our chamber.
A little water clears us of this deed;
How easy is it then! Your constancy
Hath left you unattended.
        Knock

                              Hark! more knocking.
Get on your nightgown, lest occasion call us   70
And show us to be watchers. Be not lost
So poorly in your thoughts.

MACBETH

> To know my deed 'twere best not know myself.
>> *Knock*
>
> Wake Duncan with thy knocking! I would thou couldst!
>> *Exeunt*

II.3
>> *Enter a Porter. Knocking within*

PORTER Here's a knocking indeed! If a man were porter of hell-gate he should have old turning the key.
>> *Knock*

> Knock, knock, knock! Who's there i'the name of Belzebub? Here's a farmer that hanged himself on the expectation of plenty. Come in time! Have napkins enow about you; here you'll sweat for't.
>> *Knock*

> Knock, knock! Who's there in the other devil's name? Faith, here's an equivocator that could swear in both the scales against either scale, who committed treason
10 enough for God's sake, yet could not equivocate to heaven. O, come in, equivocator.
>> *Knock*

> Knock, knock, knock! Who's there? Faith, here's an English tailor come hither for stealing out of a French hose. Come in, tailor; here you may roast your goose.
>> *Knock*

> Knock, knock! Never at quiet! What are you? – But this place is too cold for hell. I'll devil-porter it no further. I had thought to have let in some of all professions that go the primrose way to the everlasting bonfire.
>> *Knock*

> Anon, anon! I pray you remember the porter.
>> *He opens the gate. Enter Macduff and Lennox*

MACDUFF

20 Was it so late, friend, ere you went to bed,

That you do lie so late?

PORTER Faith, sir, we were carousing till the second
cock; and drink, sir, is a great provoker of three things.

MACDUFF What three things does drink especially pro-
voke?

PORTER Marry, sir, nose-painting, sleep, and urine.
Lechery, sir, it provokes and unprovokes: it provokes
the desire but it takes away the performance. Therefore
much drink may be said to be an equivocator with
lechery· it makes him and it mars him; it sets him on and 30
it takes him off; it persuades him and disheartens him,
makes him stand to and not stand to; in conclusion, equivocates him in a sleep and giving him the lie, leaves him.

MACDUFF I believe drink gave thee the lie last night.

PORTER That it did, sir, i'the very throat on me. But I
requited him for his lie and, I think, being too strong
for him, though he took up my legs sometime, yet I
made a shift to cast him.

MACDUFF Is thy master stirring?

Enter Macbeth

Our knocking has awaked him; here he comes.   40

LENNOX
Good morrow, noble sir.

MACBETH   Good morrow both.

MACDUFF
Is the King stirring, worthy thane?

MACBETH   Not yet.

MACDUFF
He did command me to call timely on him.
I have almost slipped the hour.

MACBETH   I'll bring you to him.

MACDUFF
I know this is a joyful trouble to you,
But yet 'tis one.

MACBETH

The labour we delight in physics pain.
This is the door.

MACDUFF   I'll make so bold to call,
For 'tis my limited service.   *Exit*

LENNOX

Goes the King hence today?

50 MACBETH   He does; he did appoint so.

LENNOX

The night has been unruly. Where we lay,
Our chimneys were blown down, and, as they say,
Lamentings heard i'the air, strange screams of death,
And prophesying, with accents terrible,
Of dire combustion and confused events
New-hatched to the woeful time. The obscure bird
Clamoured the live-long night. Some say the earth
Was feverous and did shake.

MACBETH   'Twas a rough night.

LENNOX

My young remembrance cannot parallel
A fellow to it.

        Enter Macduff

60 MACDUFF   O horror, horror, horror!
Tongue nor heart cannot conceive nor name thee!

MACBETH *and* LENNOX

What's the matter?

MACDUFF

Confusion now hath made his masterpiece;
Most sacrilegious murder hath broke ope
The Lord's anointed temple and stole thence
The life o'the building.

MACBETH   What is't you say? The life?

LENNOX

Mean you his majesty?

MACDUFF

    Approach the chamber and destroy your sight
    With a new Gorgon. Do not bid me speak.
    See, and then speak yourselves.

                    Exeunt Macbeth and Lennox
                          Awake, awake!   70

    Ring the alarum bell! Murder and treason!
    Banquo and Donalbain, Malcolm, awake!
    Shake off this downy sleep, death's counterfeit,
    And look on death itself! Up, up, and see
    The Great Doom's image! Malcolm, Banquo,
    As from your graves rise up and walk like sprites
    To countenance this horror. Ring the bell!

    Bell rings
    Enter Lady Macbeth

LADY

    What's the business,
    That such a hideous trumpet calls to parley
    The sleepers of the house? Speak, speak!

MACDUFF   O gentle lady,   80

    'Tis not for you to hear what I can speak.
    The repetition in a woman's ear
    Would murder as it fell.

    Enter Banquo

                    O Banquo, Banquo!
    Our royal master's murdered.

LADY   Woe, alas!

    What, in our house!

BANQUO   Too cruel, anywhere.

    Dear Duff, I prithee contradict thyself
    And say it is not so.

    Enter Macbeth, Lennox, and Ross

MACBETH

    Had I but died an hour before this chance

I had lived a blessèd time; for from this instant
90 There's nothing serious in mortality.
All is but toys, renown and grace is dead,
The wine of life is drawn, and the mere lees
Is left this vault to brag of.
Enter Malcolm and Donalbain

DONALBAIN
What is amiss?

MACBETH You are, and do not know't.
The spring, the head, the fountain of your blood
Is stopped, the very source of it is stopped.

MACDUFF
Your royal father's murdered.

MALCOLM O, by whom?

LENNOX
Those of his chamber, as it seemed, had done't:
Their hands and faces were all badged with blood,
100 So were their daggers, which, unwiped, we found
Upon their pillows; they stared and were distracted;
No man's life was to be trusted with them.

MACBETH
O yet I do repent me of my fury,
That I did kill them.

MACDUFF Wherefore did you so?

MACBETH
Who can be wise, amazed, temperate and furious,
Loyal and neutral, in a moment? No man.
The expedition of my violent love
Outrun the pauser reason. Here lay Duncan,
His silver skin laced with his golden blood,
110 And his gashed stabs looked like a breach in nature
For ruin's wasteful entrance; there the murderers,
Steeped in the colours of their trade, their daggers
Unmannerly breeched with gore. Who could refrain,

That had a heart to love, and in that heart
Courage to make's love known?

LADY (*swooning*)   Help me hence, ho!

MACDUFF
Look to the lady!

MALCOLM (*to Donalbain*)   Why do we hold our tongues,
That most may claim this argument for ours?

DONALBAIN (*to Malcolm*)
What should be spoken here where our fate,
Hid in an auger-hole, may rush and seize us?
Let's away. Our tears are not yet brewed.   120

MALCOLM (*to Donalbain*)
Nor our strong sorrow upon the foot of motion.

BANQUO
Look to the lady!
     Lady Macbeth is taken out
And when we have our naked frailties hid
That suffer in exposure, let us meet
And question this most bloody piece of work
To know it further. Fears and scruples shake us.
In the great hand of God I stand, and thence
Against the undivulged pretence I fight
Of treasonous malice.

MACDUFF   And so do I.

ALL   So all.

MACBETH
Let's briefly put on manly readiness,   130
And meet i'the hall together.

ALL   Well contented.
     Exeunt all but Malcolm and Donalbain

MALCOLM
What will you do? Let's not consort with them.
To show an unfelt sorrow is an office
Which the false man does easy. I'll to England.

DONALBAIN

> To Ireland, I. Our separated fortune
> Shall keep us both the safer. Where we are
> There's daggers in men's smiles. The nea'er in blood
> The nearer bloody.

MALCOLM   This murderous shaft that's shot

> Hath not yet lighted; and our safest way
140 Is to avoid the aim. Therefore to horse,
> And let us not be dainty of leave-taking
> But shift away. There's warrant in that theft
> Which steals itself when there's no mercy left.   *Exeunt*

II.4   *Enter Ross with an Old Man*

OLD MAN

> Threescore and ten I can remember well;
> Within the volume of which time I have seen
> Hours dreadful and things strange; but this sore night
> Hath trifled former knowings.

ROSS   Ha, good father,

> Thou seest the heavens, as troubled with man's act,
> Threatens his bloody stage. By the clock 'tis day,
> And yet dark night strangles the travelling lamp;
> Is't night's predominance or the day's shame
> That darkness does the face of earth entomb
> When living light should kiss it?

10 OLD MAN   'Tis unnatural,

> Even like the deed that's done. On Tuesday last,
> A falcon towering in her pride of place
> Was by a mousing owl hawked at and killed.

ROSS

> And Duncan's horses – a thing most strange and cer-
>   tain –
> Beauteous and swift, the minions of their race,

Turned wild in nature, broke their stalls, flung out,
Contending 'gainst obedience, as they would
Make war with mankind.

OLD MAN   'Tis said they ate each other.

ROSS

They did so, to the amazement of mine eyes
That looked upon't.

    Enter Macduff

               Here comes the good Macduff.   20
How goes the world, sir, now?

MACDUFF   Why, see you not?

ROSS

Is't known who did this more than bloody deed?

MACDUFF

Those that Macbeth hath slain.

ROSS   Alas the day!
What good could they pretend?

MACDUFF   They were suborned.
Malcolm and Donalbain, the King's two sons,
Are stolen away and fled, which puts upon them
Suspicion of the deed.

ROSS   'Gainst nature still!
Thriftless ambition that will raven up
Thine own life's means! – Then 'tis most like
The sovereignty will fall upon Macbeth?   30

MACDUFF

He is already named and gone to Scone
To be invested.

ROSS   Where is Duncan's body?

MACDUFF

Carried to Colmekill,
The sacred storehouse of his predecessors
And guardian of their bones.

ROSS   Will you to Scone?

MACDUFF
No, cousin, I'll to Fife.

ROSS   Well, I will thither.

MACDUFF
Well, may you see things well done there – Adieu! –
Lest our old robes sit easier than our new.

ROSS
Farewell, father.

OLD MAN
40   God's benison go with you, and with those
That would make good of bad, and friends of foes!

Exeunt

*

III.1   *Enter Banquo*

BANQUO
Thou hast it now: King, Cawdor, Glamis, all
As the weird women promised; and I fear
Thou playedst most foully for't. Yet it was said
It should not stand in thy posterity
But that myself should be the root and father
Of many kings. If there come truth from them,
As upon thee, Macbeth, their speeches shine,
Why by the verities on thee made good
May they not be my oracles as well
10   And set me up in hope? But hush! No more.
        *Sennet sounded. Enter Macbeth as King, Lady Mac-
        beth, Lennox, Ross, Lords, and Attendants*

MACBETH
Here's our chief guest.

LADY   If he had been forgotten
It had been as a gap in our great feast
And all-thing unbecoming.

86

MACBETH

    Tonight we hold a solemn supper, sir,
    And I'll request your presence.

BANQUO   Let your highness

    Command upon me, to the which my duties
    Are with a most indissoluble tie
    Forever knit.

MACBETH

    Ride you this afternoon?

BANQUO   Ay, my good lord.

MACBETH

    We should have else desired your good advice,   20
    Which still hath been both grave and prosperous,
    In this day's council; but we'll take tomorrow.
    Is't far you ride?

BANQUO

    As far, my lord, as will fill up the time
    'Twixt this and supper. Go not my horse the better,
    I must become a borrower of the night
    For a dark hour or twain.

MACBETH   Fail not our feast.

BANQUO

    My lord, I will not.

MACBETH

    We hear our bloody cousins are bestowed
    In England and in Ireland, not confessing   30
    Their cruel parricide, filling their hearers
    With strange invention. But of that tomorrow,
    When therewithal we shall have cause of state
    Craving us jointly. Hie you to horse. Adieu
    Till you return at night. Goes Fleance with you?

BANQUO

    Ay, my good lord; our time does call upon's.

MACBETH

    I wish your horses swift and sure of foot;

87

And so I do commend you to their backs.
Farewell.   *Exit Banquo*
40 Let every man be master of his time
Till seven at night.
To make society the sweeter welcome,
We will keep ourself till supper-time alone.
While then, God be with you!
                    Exeunt Lords and Lady Macbeth
                              Sirrah!
A word with you. Attend those men our pleasure?
SERVANT
They are, my lord, without the palace gate.
MACBETH
Bring them before us.   *Exit Servant*
                    To be thus is nothing;
But to be safely thus! – Our fears in Banquo
Stick deep; and in his royalty of nature
50 Reigns that which would be feared. 'Tis much he dares,
And to that dauntless temper of his mind
He hath a wisdom that doth guide his valour
To act in safety. There is none but he
Whose being I do fear; and under him
My genius is rebuked as, it is said,
Mark Antony's was by Caesar. He chid the sisters
When first they put the name of king upon me,
And bade them speak to him. Then, prophet-like,
They hailed him father to a line of kings.
60 Upon my head they placed a fruitless crown
And put a barren sceptre in my grip,
Thence to be wrenched with an unlineal hand,
No son of mine succeeding. If it be so,
For Banquo's issue have I filed my mind,
For them the gracious Duncan have I murdered,
Put rancours in the vessel of my peace,

Only for them; and mine eternal jewel
Given to the common enemy of man,
To make them kings, the seeds of Banquo kings!
Rather than so, come fate into the list   70
And champion me to the utterance! Who's there?

Enter Servant and two Murderers

Now go to the door, and stay there till we call. *Exit Servant*
Was it not yesterday we spoke together?

MURDERERS

It was, so please your highness.

MACBETH   Well then now,
Have you considered of my speeches? Know
That it was he in the times past which held you
So under fortune, which you thought had been
Our innocent self. This I made good to you
In our last conference; passed in probation with you
How you were borne in hand, how crossed, the
                instruments,   80
Who wrought with them, and all things else that might
To half a soul and to a notion crazed
Say, 'Thus did Banquo.'

FIRST MURDERER   You made it known to us.

MACBETH

I did so; and went further, which is now
Our point of second meeting. Do you find
Your patience so predominant in your nature
That you can let this go? Are you so gospelled,
To pray for this good man and for his issue,
Whose heavy hand hath bowed you to the grave,
And beggared yours for ever?

FIRST MURDERER   We are men, my liege.   90

MACBETH

Ay, in the catalogue ye go for men,
As hounds and greyhounds, mongrels, spaniels, curs,

Shoughs, water-rugs, and demi-wolves are clept
All by the name of dogs. The valued file
Distinguishes the swift, the slow, the subtle,
The house-keeper, the hunter, every one
According to the gift which bounteous nature
Hath in him closed; whereby he does receive
Particular addition from the bill
100   That writes them all alike. And so of men.
Now, if you have a station in the file,
Not i'the worst rank of manhood, say't,
And I will put that business in your bosoms,
Whose execution takes your enemy off,
Grapples you to the heart and love of us,
Who wear our health but sickly in his life,
Which in his death were perfect.

SECOND MURDERER   I am one, my liege,
Whom the vile blows and buffets of the world
Hath so incensed that I am reckless what I do
To spite the world.

110 FIRST MURDERER   And I another,
So weary with disasters, tugged with fortune,
That I would set my life on any chance
To mend it or be rid on't.

MACBETH   Both of you
Know Banquo was your enemy.

MURDERERS   True, my lord.

MACBETH
So is he mine, and in such bloody distance
That every minute of his being thrusts
Against my near'st of life; and though I could
With bare-faced power sweep him from my sight
And bid my will avouch it, yet I must not,
120   For certain friends that are both his and mine,
Whose loves I may not drop, but wail his fall
Who I myself struck down. And thence it is

That I to your assistance do make love,
Masking the business from the common eye
For sundry weighty reasons.

SECOND MURDERER   We shall, my lord,
Perform what you command us.

FIRST MURDERER   Though our lives –

MACBETH
Your spirits shine through you. Within this hour, at
     most,
I will advise you where to plant yourselves,
Acquaint you with the perfect spy o'the time,
The moment on't; for't must be done tonight;   130
And something from the palace; always thought
That I require a clearness; and with him,
To leave no rubs nor botches in the work,
Fleance his son, that keeps him company,
Whose absence is no less material to me
Than is his father's, must embrace the fate
Of that dark hour. Resolve yourselves apart;
I'll come to you anon.

MURDERERS   We are resolved, my lord.

MACBETH
I'll call upon you straight. Abide within.

Exeunt Murderers

It is concluded! Banquo, thy soul's flight,   140
If it find heaven, must find it out tonight.   *Exit*

Enter Macbeth's Lady and a Servant   III.2

LADY
Is Banquo gone from court?

SERVANT
Ay, madam, but returns again tonight.

LADY
Say to the King I would attend his leisure

For a few words.

SERVANT   Madam, I will.   *Exit*

LADY   Naught's had, all's spent,
Where our desire is got without content.
'Tis safer to be that which we destroy
Than by destruction dwell in doubtful joy.
     Enter Macbeth
How now, my lord? Why do you keep alone,
Of sorriest fancies your companions making,
10   Using those thoughts which should indeed have died
With them they think on? Things without all remedy
Should be without regard; what's done is done.

MACBETH
We have scorched the snake, not killed it;
She'll close and be herself, whilst our poor malice
Remains in danger of her former tooth.
But let the frame of things disjoint, both the worlds
     suffer
Ere we will eat our meal in fear, and sleep
In the affliction of these terrible dreams
That shake us nightly; better be with the dead
20   Whom we, to gain our peace, have sent to peace,
Than on the torture of the mind to lie
In restless ecstasy. Duncan is in his grave;
After life's fitful fever he sleeps well;
Treason has done his worst. Nor steel, nor poison,
Malice domestic, foreign levy, nothing
Can touch him further.

LADY   Come on,
Gentle my lord, sleek o'er your rugged looks,
Be bright and jovial among your guests tonight.

MACBETH
So shall I, love; and so I pray be you.
30   Let your remembrance apply to Banquo,

Present him eminence both with eye and tongue.
Unsafe the while that we
Must lave our honours in these flattering streams,
And make our faces vizards to our hearts,
Disguising what they are.

LADY   You must leave this.

MACBETH

O, full of scorpions is my mind, dear wife!
Thou know'st that Banquo and his Fleance lives.

LADY

But in them nature's copy's not eterne.

MACBETH

There's comfort yet! They are assailable.
Then be thou jocund. Ere the bat hath flown   40
His cloistered flight, ere to black Hecat's summons
The shard-borne beetle, with his drowsy hums,
Hath rung night's yawning peal, there shall be done
A deed of dreadful note.

LADY   What's to be done?

MACBETH

Be innocent of the knowledge, dearest chuck,
Till thou applaud the deed. Come, seeling night,
Scarf up the tender eye of pitiful day,
And with thy bloody and invisible hand
Cancel and tear to pieces that great bond
Which keeps me pale. Light thickens   50
And the crow makes wing to the rooky wood;
Good things of day begin to droop and drowse,
Whiles night's black agents to their preys do rouse.
Thou marvell'st at my words; but hold thee still.
Things bad begun make strong themselves by ill.
So, prithee, go with me.   *Exeunt*

Enter three Murderers

FIRST MURDERER

But who did bid thee join with us?

THIRD MURDERER   Macbeth.

SECOND MURDERER

He needs not our mistrust, since he delivers
Our offices and what we have to do
To the direction just.

FIRST MURDERER   Then stand with us;
The west yet glimmers with some streaks of day.
Now spurs the lated traveller apace
To gain the timely inn; and near approaches
The subject of our watch.

THIRD MURDERER   Hark, I hear horses!

BANQUO (*within*)

Give us a light there, ho!

SECOND MURDERER   Then 'tis he.

10   The rest that are within the note of expectation,
Already are i'the court.

FIRST MURDERER   His horses go about.

THIRD MURDERER

Almost a mile; but he does usually.
So all men do, from hence to the palace gate
Make it their walk.

Enter Banquo and Fleance, with a torch

SECOND MURDERER

A light, a light!

THIRD MURDERER

'Tis he.

FIRST MURDERER   Stand to't!

BANQUO

It will be rain tonight.

FIRST MURDERER   Let it come down!

They attack Banquo

BANQUO

  O treachery! Fly, good Fleance, fly, fly, fly!
  Thou mayst revenge – O slave!

    Banquo falls. Fleance escapes

THIRD MURDERER

  Who did strike out the light?

FIRST MURDERER   Was't not the way?

THIRD MURDERER

  There's but one down; the son is fled.

SECOND MURDERER   We have lost   20

  Best half of our affair.

FIRST MURDERER

  Well, let's away and say how much is done.   *Exeunt*

    Banquet prepared. Enter Macbeth, Lady Macbeth, III 4
    Ross, Lennox, Lords, and Attendants

MACBETH

  You know your own degrees, sit down. At first
  And last, the hearty welcome.

LORDS   Thanks to your majesty.

MACBETH

  Ourself will mingle with society
  And play the humble host.

    He walks around the tables

  Our hostess keeps her state; but in best time
  We will require her welcome.

LADY

  Pronounce it for me, sir, to all our friends,
  For my heart speaks they are welcome.

    Enter First Murderer

MACBETH

  See, they encounter thee with their hearts' thanks;
  Both sides are even. Here I'll sit i'the midst.   10

Be large in mirth. Anon we'll drink a measure
The table round.
> *He rises and goes to the Murderer*

There's blood upon thy face!

FIRST MURDERER

'Tis Banquo's then.

MACBETH

'Tis better thee without than he within.
Is he dispatched?

FIRST MURDERER My lord, his throat is cut;
That I did for him.

MACBETH   Thou art the best o'the cut-throats.
Yet he's good that did the like for Fleance.
If thou didst it, thou art the nonpareil.

FIRST MURDERER

Most royal sir – Fleance is scaped.

MACBETH

20 Then comes my fit again. I had else been perfect,
Whole as the marble, founded as the rock,
As broad and general as the casing air;
But now I am cabined, cribbed, confined, bound in
To saucy doubts and fears. – But Banquo's safe?

FIRST MURDERER

Ay, my good lord; safe in a ditch he bides,
With twenty trenchèd gashes on his head,
The least a death to nature.

MACBETH   Thanks for that.
There the grown serpent lies. The worm that's fled
Hath nature that in time will venom breed,
30 No teeth for the present. Get thee gone. Tomorrow
We'll hear ourselves again.   *Exit Murderer*

LADY   My royal lord,
You do not give the cheer. The feast is sold
That is not often vouched, while 'tis a-making,

'Tis given with welcome. To feed were best at home;
From thence, the sauce to meat is ceremony;
Meeting were bare without it.

MACBETH   Sweet remembrancer!
Now good digestion wait on appetite,
And health on both!

LENNOX   May't please your highness sit.

Enter the Ghost of Banquo and sits in Macbeth's place

MACBETH
Here had we now our country's honour roofed,
Were the graced person of our Banquo present;   40
Who may I rather challenge for unkindness
Than pity for mischance.

ROSS   His absence, sir,
Lays blame upon his promise. Please't your highness
To grace us with your royal company?

MACBETH
The table's full.

LENNOX   Here is a place reserved, sir.

MACBETH
Where?

LENNOX
Here, my good lord. What is't that moves your highness?

MACBETH
Which of you have done this?

LORDS   What, my good lord?

MACBETH
Thou canst not say I did it; never shake
Thy gory locks at me.   50

ROSS
Gentlemen, rise. His highness is not well.

LADY (*descends from her throne*)
Sit, worthy friends. My lord is often thus;
And hath been from his youth. Pray you keep seat.

The fit is momentary; upon a thought
He will again be well. If much you note him,
You shall offend him and extend his passion.
Feed, and regard him not. – Are you a man?

MACBETH

Ay, and a bold one, that dare look on that
Which might appal the devil.

LADY   O proper stuff!

60 This is the very painting of your fear.
This is the air-drawn dagger which you said
Led you to Duncan. O, these flaws and starts,
Impostors to true fear, would well become
A woman's story at a winter's fire,
Authorized by her grandam. Shame itself!
Why do you make such faces? When all's done
You look but on a stool.

MACBETH   Prithee, see there!
Behold! Look! Lo! – How say you?
Why, what care I if thou canst nod! Speak, too!

70 If charnel-houses and our graves must send
Those that we bury, back, our monuments
Shall be the maws of kites.   *Exit Ghost*

LADY   What, quite unmanned in folly?

MACBETH

If I stand here, I saw him.

LADY   Fie, for shame!

MACBETH

Blood hath been shed ere now, i'the olden time,
Ere humane statute purged the gentle weal;
Ay, and since too, murders have been performed
Too terrible for the ear. The times has been
That, when the brains were out, the man would die,
And there an end. But now they rise again

80 With twenty mortal murders on their crowns,

98

And push us from our stools. This is more strange
Than such a murder is.

LADY   My worthy lord,
Your noble friends do lack you.

MACBETH   I do forget.
Do not muse at me, my most worthy friends:
I have a strange infirmity, which is nothing
To those that know me. Come, love and health to all!
Then I'll sit down. Give me some wine; fill full!

    Enter Ghost

I drink to the general joy o'the whole table,
And to our dear friend Banquo, whom we miss.
Would he were here! To all – and him – we thirst,   90
And all to all.

LORDS   Our duties and the pledge!

MACBETH (*sees the Ghost*)
Avaunt, and quit my sight! Let the earth hide thee!
Thy bones are marrowless, thy blood is cold.
Thou hast no speculation in those eyes
Which thou dost glare with.

LADY   Think of this, good peers,
But as a thing of custom; 'tis no other;
Only it spoils the pleasure of the time.

MACBETH
What man dare, I dare.
Approach thou like the rugged Russian bear,
The armed rhinoceros, or the Hyrcan tiger,   100
Take any shape but that, and my firm nerves
Shall never tremble. Or be alive again,
And dare me to the desert with thy sword:
If trembling I inhabit then, protest me
The baby of a girl. Hence, horrible shadow!
Unreal mockery, hence!   *Exit Ghost*
            Why, so; being gone,

I am a man again. – Pray you sit still.

LADY

You have displaced the mirth, broke the good meeting
With most admired disorder.

MACBETH   Can such things be,
110 And overcome us like a summer's cloud,
Without our special wonder? You make me strange
Even to the disposition that I owe
When now I think you can behold such sights
And keep the natural ruby of your cheeks,
When mine is blanched with fear.

ROSS   What sights, my lord?

LADY

I pray you speak not; he grows worse and worse.
Question enrages him. At once, good night.
Stand not upon the order of your going;
But go at once.

LENNOX   Good night; and better health
Attend his majesty!

120 LADY   A kind good-night to all!   *Exeunt Lords*

MACBETH

It will have blood, they say; blood will have blood.
Stones have been known to move and trees to speak;
Augurs and understood relations have
By maggot-pies, and choughs, and rooks brought forth
The secret'st man of blood. What is the night?

LADY

Almost at odds with morning, which is which.

MACBETH

How sayst thou, that Macduff denies his person
At our great bidding?

LADY   Did you send to him, sir?

MACBETH

I hear it by the way. But I will send.

There's not a one of them, but in his house   130
I keep a servant fee'd. I will tomorrow –
And betimes I will – to the Weird Sisters.
More shall they speak; for now I am bent to know
By the worst means the worst. For mine own good
All causes shall give way. I am in blood
Stepped in so far, that, should I wade no more,
Returning were as tedious as go o'er.
Strange things I have in head, that will to hand;
Which must be acted ere they may be scanned.

LADY

You lack the season of all natures, sleep.   140

MACBETH

Come, we'll to sleep. My strange and self-abuse
Is the initiate fear that wants hard use.
We are yet but young in deed.   *Exeunt*

Thunder. Enter the three Witches, meeting Hecat   III.5

FIRST WITCH

Why, how now, Hecat? You look angerly.

HECAT

Have I not reason, beldams, as you are
Saucy and over-bold? How did you dare
To trade and traffic with Macbeth
In riddles and affairs of death,
And I, the mistress of your charms,
The close contriver of all harms,
Was never called to bear my part,
Or show the glory of our art?
And, which is worse, all you have done   10
Hath been but for a wayward son,
Spiteful and wrathful, who, as others do,
Loves for his own ends, not for you.

But make amends now: get you gone,
And at the pit of Acheron
Meet me i'the morning. Thither he
Will come, to know his destiny.
Your vessels and your spells provide,
Your charms and everything beside.
20 I am for the air; this night I'll spend
Unto a dismal and a fatal end.
Great business must be wrought ere noon
Upon the corner of the moon:
There, hangs a vaporous drop profound;
I'll catch it ere it come to ground;
And that distilled by magic sleights
Shall raise such artificial sprites
As by the strength of their illusion
Shall draw him on to his confusion.
30 He shall spurn fate, scorn death, and bear
His hopes 'bove wisdom, grace, and fear.
And you all know security
Is mortals' chiefest enemy.
        Music and a song
Hark! I am called. My little spirit, see,
Sits in a foggy cloud and stays for me.
        Sing within: 'Come away, come away,' etc.

FIRST WITCH
Come, let's make haste; she'll soon be back again.
        Exeunt

III.6   *Enter Lennox and another Lord*
LENNOX
My former speeches have but hit your thoughts,
Which can interpret further. Only I say
Things have been strangely borne. The gracious Duncan

Was pitied of Macbeth: marry, he was dead!
And the right valiant Banquo walked too late;
Whom you may say, if't please you, Fleance killed,
For Fleance fled. Men must not walk too late.
Who cannot want the thought how monstrous
It was for Malcolm and for Donalbain
To kill their gracious father? Damnèd fact,   10
How it did grieve Macbeth! Did he not straight –
In pious rage – the two delinquents tear,
That were the slaves of drink, and thralls of sleep?
Was not that nobly done? Ay, and wisely too;
For 'twould have angered any heart alive
To hear the men deny't. So that I say
He has borne all things well; and I do think
That had he Duncan's sons under his key –
As, an't please heaven, he shall not – they should find
What 'twere to kill a father – so should Fleance.   20
But, peace! For from broad words, and 'cause he failed
His presence at the tyrant's feast, I hear
Macduff lives in disgrace. Sir, can you tell
Where he bestows himself?

LORD   The son of Duncan,
From whom this tyrant holds the due of birth,
Lives in the English court, and is received
Of the most pious Edward with such grace
That the malevolence of fortune nothing
Takes from his high respect. Thither Macduff
Is gone to pray the holy king, upon his aid,   30
To wake Northumberland and warlike Seyward,
That by the help of these – with Him above
To ratify the work – we may again
Give to our tables meat, sleep to our nights,
Free from our feasts and banquets bloody knives,
Do faithful homage and receive free honours –

All which we pine for now. And this report
Hath so exasperate the King that he
Prepares for some attempt of war.

LENNOX   Sent he to Macduff?

LORD

40 He did. And with an absolute 'Sir, not I!'
The cloudy messenger turns me his back
And hums, as who should say 'You'll rue the time
That clogs me with this answer.'

LENNOX   And that well might
Advise him to a caution to hold what distance
His wisdom can provide. Some holy angel
Fly to the court of England and unfold
His message ere he come, that a swift blessing
May soon return to this our suffering country,
Under a hand accursed!

LORD   I'll send my prayers with him.

                                                        Exeunt

*

IV.1   *Thunder. Enter the three Witches*

FIRST WITCH

          Thrice the brinded cat hath mewed.

SECOND WITCH

          Thrice, and once the hedge-pig whined.

THIRD WITCH

          Harpier cries! 'Tis time, 'tis time!

FIRST WITCH

          Round about the cauldron go;
          In the poisoned entrails throw:
          Toad that under cold stone
          Days and nights has thirty-one.

Sweltered venom, sleeping got,
Boil thou first i'the charmèd pot.

ALL

Double, double, toil and trouble;   10
Fire burn, and cauldron bubble.

SECOND WITCH

Fillet of a fenny snake
In the cauldron boil and bake;
Eye of newt, and toe of frog,
Wool of bat, and tongue of dog,
Adder's fork, and blind-worm's sting,
Lizard's leg and howlet's wing,
For a charm of powerful trouble,
Like a hell-broth, boil and bubble.

ALL

Double, double, toil and trouble;   20
Fire burn, and cauldron bubble.

THIRD WITCH

Scale of dragon, tooth of wolf,
Witch's mummy, maw and gulf
Of the ravined salt sea shark,
Root of hemlock digged i'the dark,
Liver of blaspheming Jew,
Gall of goat, and slips of yew
Slivered in the moon's eclipse,
Nose of Turk, and Tartar's lips,
Finger of birth-strangled babe,   30
Ditch-delivered by a drab,
Make the gruel thick and slab.
Add thereto a tiger's chaudron
For the ingredience of our cauldron.

ALL

Double, double, toil and trouble;
Fire burn, and cauldron bubble.

SECOND WITCH

>Cool it with a baboon's blood;
>Then the charm is firm and good.

Enter Hecat and the other three Witches

HECAT

>O well done! I commend your pains;
>And everyone shall share i'the gains.
>And now about the cauldron sing
>Like elves and fairies in a ring,
>Enchanting all that you put in.

Music and a song: 'Black spirits' etc.

>>*Exeunt Hecat and the other three Witches*

SECOND WITCH

>By the pricking of my thumbs,
>Something wicked this way comes.
>Open, locks, whoever knocks!

Enter Macbeth

MACBETH

How now, you secret, black, and midnight hags!
What is't you do?

ALL   A deed without a name.

MACBETH

I conjure you, by that which you profess,
Howe'er you come to know it, answer me –
Though you untie the winds and let them fight
Against the churches; though the yesty waves
Confound and swallow navigation up;
Though bladed corn be lodged and trees blown down;
Though castles topple on their warders' heads;
Though palaces and pyramids do slope
Their heads to their foundations; though the treasure
Of nature's germens tumble all together
Even till destruction sicken – answer me
To what I ask you.

FIRST WITCH   Speak.
SECOND WITCH   Demand.
THIRD WITCH   We'll answer.   60
FIRST WITCH
    Say if thou'dst rather hear it from our mouths
    Or from our masters.
MACBETH   Call 'em. Let me see 'em.
FIRST WITCH
            Pour in sow's blood that hath eaten
            Her nine farrow; grease that's sweaten
            From the murderer's gibbet, throw
            Into the flame.
ALL   Come high or low,
            Thyself and office deftly show.
        Thunder. First Apparition, an Armed Head
MACBETH
    Tell me, thou unknown power –
FIRST WITCH   He knows thy thought.
    Hear his speech, but say thou naught.
FIRST APPARITION
    Macbeth, Macbeth, Macbeth, beware Macduff!   70
    Beware the Thane of Fife! Dismiss me. Enough.
                                    He descends
MACBETH
    Whate'er thou art, for thy good caution, thanks;
    Thou hast harped my fear aright. But one word more –
FIRST WITCH
    He will not be commanded. Here's another
    More potent than the first.
        Thunder. Second Apparition, a Bloody Child
SECOND APPARITION
    Macbeth, Macbeth, Macbeth!
MACBETH
    Had I three ears, I'd hear thee.

SECOND APPARITION

Be bloody, bold, and resolute; laugh to scorn
The power of man; for none of woman born
80   Shall harm Macbeth.   *He descends*

MACBETH

Then live Macduff; what need I fear of thee?
But yet I'll make assurance double sure,
And take a bond of fate. Thou shalt not live;
That I may tell pale-hearted fear it lies,
And sleep in spite of thunder.

> *Thunder. Third Apparition, a Child crowned, with a
> tree in his hand*

                                        What is this
That rises like the issue of a king,
And wears upon his baby brow the round
And top of sovereignty?

ALL   Listen, but speak not to't.

THIRD APPARITION

Be lion-mettled, proud, and take no care
90   Who chafes, who frets, or where conspirers are;
Macbeth shall never vanquished be, until
Great Birnan Wood to high Dunsinane Hill
Shall come against him.   *He descends*

MACBETH   That will never be.
Who can impress the forest, bid the tree
Unfix his earth-bound root? Sweet bodements! Good!
Rebellious dead rise never till the wood
Of Birnan rise, and our high-placed Macbeth
Shall live the lease of nature, pay his breath
To time and mortal custom. Yet my heart
100   Throbs to know one thing: tell me, if your art
Can tell so much, shall Banquo's issue ever
Reign in this kingdom?

ALL   Seek to know no more.

MACBETH

    I will be satisfied! Deny me this
    And an eternal curse fall on you! Let me know.
    Why sinks that cauldron?
       Hautboys

                        And what noise is this?

FIRST WITCH
    Show!

SECOND WITCH
    Show!

THIRD WITCH
    Show!

ALL

        Show his eyes and grieve his heart;
        Come like shadows, so depart.   110
        A show of eight kings, and Banquo; the last king with
        a glass in his hand

MACBETH

    Thou art too like the spirit of Banquo. Down!
    Thy crown does sear mine eye-balls. And thy hair,
    Thou other gold-bound brow, is like the first.
    A third is like the former. – Filthy hags,
    Why do you show me this? – A fourth? Start, eyes!
    What, will the line stretch out to the crack of doom?
    Another yet? A seventh? I'll see no more!
    And yet the eighth appears, who bears a glass
    Which shows me many more. And some I see
    That two-fold balls and treble sceptres carry.   120
    Horrible sight! Now I see 'tis true,
    For the blood-boltered Banquo smiles upon me,
    And points at them for his. What! Is this so?

FIRST WITCH

        Ay, sir, all this is so. But why
        Stands Macbeth thus amazedly?

> Come, sisters, cheer we up his sprites
> And show the best of our delights.
> I'll charm the air to give a sound,
> While you perform your antic round,
> 130   That this great king may kindly say
> Our duties did his welcome pay.

Music. The Witches dance; and vanish

MACBETH

Where are they? Gone! Let this pernicious hour
Stand aye accursèd in the calendar.
Come in, without there.

Enter Lennox

LENNOX   What's your grace's will?

MACBETH

Saw you the Weird Sisters?

LENNOX   No, my lord.

MACBETH

Came they not by you?

LENNOX   No, indeed, my lord.

MACBETH

Infected be the air whereon they ride,
And damned all those that trust them. I did hear
The galloping of horse. Who was't came by?

LENNOX

140   'Tis two or three, my lord, that bring you word
Macduff is fled to England.

MACBETH   Fled to England!

LENNOX

Ay, my good lord.

MACBETH

Time, thou anticipat'st my dread exploits.
The flighty purpose never is o'ertook
Unless the deed go with it. From this moment
The very firstlings of my heart shall be
The firstlings of my hand. And even now,

To crown my thoughts with acts, be it thought and done:
The castle of Macduff I will surprise,
Seize upon Fife, give to the edge o'the sword   150
His wife, his babes, and all unfortunate souls
That trace him in his line. No boasting, like a fool;
This deed I'll do before this purpose cool.
But no more sights! – Where are these gentlemen?
Come, bring me where they are.

                                        Exeunt

Enter Macduff's Wife, her Son, and Ross   IV.2

WIFE
What had he done to make him fly the land?
ROSS
You must have patience, madam.
WIFE   He had none.
His flight was madness; when our actions do not,
Our fears do make us traitors.
ROSS   You know not
Whether it was his wisdom or his fear.
WIFE
Wisdom! To leave his wife, to leave his babes,
His mansion and his titles, in a place
From whence himself does fly? He loves us not.
He wants the natural touch; for the poor wren,
The most diminutive of birds, will fight,   10
Her young ones in her nest, against the owl.
All is the fear and nothing is the love,
As little is the wisdom, where the flight
So runs against all reason.
ROSS   My dearest cuz,
I pray you school yourself. But, for your husband,
He is noble, wise, judicious, and best knows
The fits o'the season. I dare not speak much further,

But cruel are the times when we are traitors
And do not know, ourselves; when we hold rumour
20 From what we fear, yet know not what we fear,
But float upon a wild and violent sea,
Each way and move. I take my leave of you;
Shall not be long but I'll be here again.
Things at the worst will cease or else climb upward
To what they were before. – My pretty cousin,
Blessing upon you!

WIFE

Fathered he is, and yet he's fatherless.

ROSS

I am so much a fool, should I stay longer
It would be my disgrace and your discomfort.
30 I take my leave at once.   *Exit*

WIFE

Sirrah, your father's dead.
And what will you do now? How will you live?

SON

As birds do, mother.

WIFE   What, with worms and flies?

SON

With what I get, I mean; and so do they.

WIFE

Poor bird, thou'dst never fear
The net nor lime, the pitfall nor the gin!

SON

Why should I, mother? Poor birds they are not set for.
My father is not dead, for all your saying.

WIFE

Yes, he is dead. How wilt thou do for a father?
40 SON Nay, how will you do for a husband?
WIFE Why, I can buy me twenty at any market.
SON Then you'll buy 'em to sell again.

WIFE

    Thou speak'st with all thy wit;

    And yet, i'faith, with wit enough for thee.

SON Was my father a traitor, mother?

WIFE Ay, that he was.

SON What is a traitor?

WIFE Why, one that swears and lies.

SON And be all traitors that do so?

WIFE

    Every one that does so is a traitor,   50

    And must be hanged.

SON

    And must they all be hanged that swear and lie?

WIFE Every one.

SON Who must ha·g them?

WIFE Why, the honest men.

SON Then the liars and swearers are fools; for there are liars and swearers enow to beat the honest men and hang up them.

WIFE Now God help thee, poor monkey! But how wilt thou do for a father?   60

SON If he were dead, you'd weep for him; if you would not, it were a good sign that I should quickly have a new father.

WIFE Poor prattler, how thou talk'st!

    Enter a Messenger

MESSENGER

    Bless you, fair dame! I am not to you known,

    Though in your state of honour I am perfect.

    I doubt some danger does approach you nearly.

    If you will take a homely man's advice,

    Be not found here. Hence with your little ones!

    To fright you thus methinks I am too savage;   70

    To do worse to you were fell cruelty,

Which is too nigh your person. Heaven preserve you!
I dare abide no longer.   *Exit*

WIFE   Whither should I fly?
I have done no harm. But I remember now
I am in this earthly world, where to do harm
Is often laudable, to do good sometime
Accounted dangerous folly. Why then, alas,
Do I put up that womanly defence
To say I have done no harm?

         Enter Murderers   What are these faces?

MURDERER
80 Where is your husband?

WIFE
    I hope in no place so unsanctified
    Where such as thou mayst find him.

MURDERER   He's a traitor.

SON
    Thou liest, thou shag-haired villain!

MURDERER   What, you egg,
    Young fry of treachery!
         He stabs him

SON   He has killed me, mother!
    Run away, I pray you.
                    Son dies. Exit Wife crying 'Murder'

IV.3   *Enter Malcolm and Macduff*

MALCOLM
    Let us seek out some desolate shade, and there
    Weep our sad bosoms empty.

MACDUFF   Let us rather
    Hold fast the mortal sword; and like good men
    Bestride our down-fallen birthdom. Each new morn
    New widows howl, new orphans cry, new sorrows

Strike heaven on the face, that it resounds
As if it felt with Scotland, and yelled out
Like syllable of dolour.

MALCOLM   What I believe, I'll wail;
What know, believe; and what I can redress,
As I shall find the time to friend, I will.   10
What you have spoke, it may be so perchance.
This tyrant, whose sole name blisters our tongues,
Was once thought honest; you have loved him well;
He hath not touched you yet. I am young; but
            something
You may deserve of him, through me; and wisdom
To offer up a weak poor innocent lamb
T'appease an angry god.

MACDUFF
I am not treacherous.

MALCOLM   But Macbeth is.
A good and virtuous nature may recoil
In an imperial charge. But I shall crave your pardon: 20
That which you are my thoughts cannot transpose;
Angels are bright still though the brightest fell.
Though all things foul would wear the brows of grace,
Yet grace must still look so.

MACDUFF   I have lost my hopes.

MALCOLM
Perchance even there where I did find my doubts.
Why in that rawness left you wife and child,
Those precious motives, those strong knots of love,
Without leave-taking? I pray you,
Let not my jealousies be your dishonours
But mine own safeties. You may be rightly just,   30
Whatever I shall think.

MACDUFF   Bleed, bleed, poor country!
Great tyranny, lay thou thy basis sure,

For goodness dare not check thee; wear thou thy wrongs,
The title is affeered. Fare thee well, lord!
I would not be the villain that thou think'st
For the whole space that's in the tyrant's grasp,
And the rich East to boot.

MALCOLM   Be not offended;
I speak not as in absolute fear of you.
I think our country sinks beneath the yoke,
40   It weeps, it bleeds, and each new day a gash
Is added to her wounds. I think withal
There would be hands uplifted in my right;
And here from gracious England have I offer
Of goodly thousands. But for all this,
When I shall tread upon the tyrant's head
Or wear it on my sword, yet my poor country
Shall have more vices than it had before,
More suffer, and more sundry ways, than ever,
By him that shall succeed.

MACDUFF   What should he be?

MALCOLM
50   It is myself I mean; in whom I know
All the particulars of vice so grafted
That, when they shall be opened, black Macbeth
Will seem as pure as snow and the poor state
Esteem him as a lamb, being compared
With my confineless harms.

MACDUFF   Not in the legions
Of horrid hell can come a devil more damned
In evils to top Macbeth.

MALCOLM   I grant him bloody,
Luxurious, avaricious, false, deceitful,
Sudden, malicious, smacking of every sin
60   That has a name. But there's no bottom, none,
In my voluptuousness. Your wives, your daughters,

Your matrons, and your maids, could not fill up
The cistern of my lust; and my desire
All continent impediments would o'erbear
That did oppose my will. Better Macbeth
Than such a one to reign.

MACDUFF   Boundless intemperance
In nature is a tyranny. It hath been
The untimely emptying of the happy throne,
And fall of many kings. But fear not yet
To take upon you what is yours. You may   70
Convey your pleasures in a spacious plenty
And yet seem cold; the time you may so hoodwink.
We have willing dames enough. There cannot be
That vulture in you to devour so many
As will to greatness dedicate themselves,
Finding it so inclined.

MALCOLM   With this there grows
In my most ill-composed affection such
A staunchless avarice that, were I king,
I should cut off the nobles for their lands,
Desire his jewels and this other's house,   80
And my more-having would be as a sauce
To make me hunger more, that I should forge
Quarrels unjust against the good and loyal,
Destroying them for wealth.

MACDUFF   This avarice
Sticks deeper, grows with more pernicious root
Than summer-seeming lust; and it hath been
The sword of our slain kings. Yet do not fear:
Scotland hath foisons to fill up your will
Of your mere own. All these are portable,
With other graces weighed.

MALCOLM   But I have none.   90
The king-becoming graces,

117

As justice, verity, temperance, stableness,
Bounty, perseverance, mercy, lowliness,
Devotion, patience, courage, fortitude,
I have no relish of them, but abound
In the division of each several crime,
Acting it many ways. Nay, had I power, I should
Pour the sweet milk of concord into hell,
Uproar the universal peace, confound
All unity on earth.

100   MACDUFF   O Scotland, Scotland!

MALCOLM
If such a one be fit to govern, speak.
I am as I have spoken.

MACDUFF   Fit to govern!
No, not to live! O nation miserable,
With an untitled tyrant, bloody-sceptred,
When shalt thou see thy wholesome days again,
Since that the truest issue of thy throne
By his own interdiction stands accused
And does blaspheme his breed? Thy royal father
Was a most sainted king; the queen that bore thee,
110   Oftener upon her knees than on her feet,
Died every day she lived. Fare thee well!
These evils thou repeat'st upon thyself
Hath banished me from Scotland. O my breast,
Thy hope ends here!

MALCOLM   Macduff, this noble passion,
Child of integrity, hath from my soul
Wiped the black scruples, reconciled my thoughts
To thy good truth and honour. Devilish Macbeth
By many of these trains hath sought to win me
Into his power, and modest wisdom plucks me
120   From over-credulous haste. But God above
Deal between thee and me; for even now

I put myself to thy direction, and
Unspeak mine own detraction, here abjure
The taints and blames I laid upon myself
For strangers to my nature. I am yet
Unknown to woman, never was forsworn,
Scarcely have coveted what was mine own,
At no time broke my faith, would not betray
The devil to his fellow, and delight
No less in truth than life. My first false speaking   130
Was this upon myself. What I am truly
Is thine and my poor country's to command;
Whither indeed, before thy here-approach,
Old Seyward with ten thousand warlike men,
Already at a point, was setting forth.
Now we'll together; and the chance of goodness
Be like our warranted quarrel! Why are you silent?

MACDUFF

Such welcome and unwelcome things at once
'Tis hard to reconcile.

    Enter a Doctor

MALCOLM   Well, more anon. –
Comes the King forth, I pray you?   140

DOCTOR

Ay, sir. There are a crew of wretched souls
That stay his cure. Their malady convinces
The great assay of art; but at his touch,
Such sanctity hath heaven given his hand,
They presently amend.

MALCOLM   I thank you, doctor.

                    Exit Doctor

MACDUFF

What's the disease he means?

MALCOLM   'Tis called the Evil –
A most miraculous work in this good king,

Which often since my here-remain in England
I have seen him do. How he solicits heaven
150   Himself best knows: but strangely visited people,
All swollen and ulcerous, pitiful to the eye,
The mere despair of surgery, he cures,
Hanging a golden stamp about their necks
Put on with holy prayers; and 'tis spoken,
To the succeeding royalty he leaves
The healing benediction. With this strange virtue
He hath a heavenly gift of prophecy,
And sundry blessings hang about his throne
That speak him full of grace.

    Enter Ross

MACDUFF   See who comes here.

MALCOLM
160   My countryman; but yet I know him not.

MACDUFF

My ever gentle cousin, welcome hither.

MALCOLM

I know him now. Good God betimes remove
The means that makes us strangers!

ROSS   Sir, amen.

MACDUFF

Stands Scotland where it did?

ROSS   Alas, poor country,
Almost afraid to know itself! It cannot
Be called our mother, but our grave; where nothing
But who knows nothing is once seen to smile;
Where sighs and groans and shrieks that rent the air
Are made, not marked; where violent sorrow seems
170   A modern ecstasy. The dead man's knell
Is there scarce asked for who, and good men's lives
Expire before the flowers in their caps,
Dying or ere they sicken.

MACDUFF   O relation
  Too nice and yet too true.
MALCOLM   What's the newest grief?
ROSS
  That of an hour's age doth hiss the speaker;
  Each minute teems a new one.
MACDUFF   How does my wife?
ROSS
  Why, well.
MACDUFF
              And all my children?
ROSS   Well too.
MACDUFF
  The tyrant has not battered at their peace?
ROSS
  No. They were well at peace when I did leave 'em.
MACDUFF
  Be not a niggard of your speech. How goes't?   180
ROSS
  When I came hither to transport the tidings
  Which I have heavily borne, there ran a rumour
  Of many worthy fellows that were out,
  Which was to my belief witnessed the rather
  For that I saw the tyrant's power afoot.
  Now is the time of help. (*To Malcolm*) Your eye in
      Scotland
  Would create soldiers, make our women fight
  To doff their dire distresses.
MALCOLM   Be't their comfort
  We are coming thither. Gracious England hath
  Lent us good Seyward and ten thousand men –   190
  An older and a better soldier none
  That Christendom gives out.
ROSS   Would I could answer

    This comfort with the like. But I have words
    That would be howled out in the desert air,
    Where hearing should not latch them.

MACDUFF   What concern they?
    The general cause, or is it a fee-grief
    Due to some single breast?

ROSS   No mind that's honest
    But in it shares some woe, though the main part
    Pertains to you alone.

MACDUFF   If it be mine,
200   Keep it not from me; quickly let me have it.

ROSS
    Let not your ears despise my tongue for ever,
    Which shall possess them with the heaviest sound
    That ever yet they heard.

MACDUFF   Humh! I guess at it.

ROSS
    Your castle is surprised, your wife and babes
    Savagely slaughtered. To relate the manner
    Were on the quarry of these murdered deer
    To add the death of you.

MALCOLM   Merciful heaven!
    What, man! Ne'er pull your hat upon your brows.
    Give sorrow words: the grief that does not speak
210   Whispers the o'erfraught heart and bids it break.

MACDUFF
    My children too?

ROSS   Wife, children, servants, all
    That could be found.

MACDUFF   And I must be from thence!
    My wife killed too?

ROSS   I have said.

MALCOLM   Be comforted.
    Let's make us medicines of our great revenge

To cure this deadly grief.

MACDUFF   He has no children.

All my pretty ones? Did you say all?
O hell-kite! All? What, all my pretty chickens
And their dam, at one fell swoop?

MALCOLM

Dispute it like a man.

MACDUFF   I shall do so;

But I must also feel it as a man.   220
I cannot but remember such things were
That were most precious to me. Did heaven look on
And would not take their part? Sinful Macduff!
They were all struck for thee. Naught that I am,
Not for their own demerits, but for mine,
Fell slaughter on their souls. Heaven rest them now!

MALCOLM

Be this the whetstone of your sword; let grief
Convert to anger; blunt not the heart, enrage it.

MACDUFF

O, I could play the woman with mine eyes
And braggart with my tongue! But, gentle heavens,   230
Cut short all intermission. Front to front
Bring thou this fiend of Scotland and myself.
Within my sword's length set him; if he scape,
Heaven forgive him too.

MALCOLM   This tune goes manly.

Come, go we to the King; our power is ready;
Our lack is nothing but our leave. Macbeth
Is ripe for shaking, and the powers above
Put on their instruments. Receive what cheer you may:
The night is long that never finds the day.   *Exeunt*

*

Enter a Doctor of Physic and a Waiting-Gentlewoman

DOCTOR I have two nights watched with you, but can
perceive no truth in your report. When was it she last
walked?

GENTLEWOMAN Since his majesty went into the field I
have seen her rise from her bed, throw her nightgown
upon her, unlock her closet, take forth paper, fold it,
write upon't, read it, afterwards seal it, and again return
to bed; yet all this while in a most fast sleep.

DOCTOR A great perturbation in nature, to receive at once
10   the benefit of sleep and do the effects of watching. In
this slumbery agitation, besides her walking and other
actual performances, what, at any time, have you heard
her say?

GENTLEWOMAN That, sir, which I will not report after
her.

DOCTOR You may to me; and 'tis most meet you should.

GENTLEWOMAN Neither to you nor anyone, having no
witness to confirm my speech.

          Enter Lady Macbeth with a taper

Lo you! Here she comes. This is her very guise; and,
20   upon my life, fast asleep. Observe her; stand close.

DOCTOR How came she by that light?

GENTLEWOMAN Why, it stood by her. She has light by
her continually; 'tis her command.

DOCTOR You see her eyes are open.

GENTLEWOMAN Ay, but their sense are shut.

DOCTOR What is it she does now? Look how she rubs her
hands.

GENTLEWOMAN It is an accustomed action with her to
seem thus washing her hands. I have known her con-
30   tinue in this a quarter of an hour.

LADY Yet here's a spot.

DOCTOR Hark! She speaks. I will set down what comes

from her, to satisfy my remembrance the more strongly.

LADY Out, damned spot! Out, I say! – One: two: why then, 'tis time to do't. – Hell is murky! – Fie, my lord, fie! A soldier and afeard? – What need we fear who knows it, when none can call our power to accompt? – Yet who would have thought the old man to have had so much blood in him?

DOCTOR Do you mark that? 40

LADY The Thane of Fife had a wife; where is she now? – What, will these hands ne'er be clean? – No more o'that, my lord, no more o'that. You mar all with this starting.

DOCTOR Go to, go to: you have known what you should not.

GENTLEWOMAN She has spoke what she should not, I am sure of that. Heaven knows what she has known.

LADY Here's the smell of the blood still. All the perfumes of Arabia will not sweeten this little hand. Oh! Oh! Oh!

DOCTOR What a sigh is there! The heart is sorely charged. 50

GENTLEWOMAN I would not have such a heart in my bosom for the dignity of the whole body.

DOCTOR Well, well, well.

GENTLEWOMAN Pray God it be, sir.

DOCTOR This disease is beyond my practice; yet I have known those which have walked in their sleep who have died holily in their beds.

LADY Wash your hands; put on your nightgown; look not so pale. I tell you yet again, Banquo's buried; he cannot come out on's grave. 60

DOCTOR Even so?

LADY To bed, to bed! There's knocking at the gate. Come, come, come, come, give me your hand. What's done cannot be undone. To bed, to bed, to bed.

Exit

DOCTOR Will she go now to bed?

125

GENTLEWOMAN Directly.

DOCTOR

Foul whisperings are abroad, unnatural deeds
Do breed unnatural troubles; infected minds
To their deaf pillows will discharge their secrets.
70   More needs she the divine than the physician.
God, God forgive us all! Look after her,
Remove from her the means of all annoyance
And still keep eyes upon her. So, good night.
My mind she has mated, and amazed my sight.
I think, but dare not speak.

GENTLEWOMAN   Good night, good doctor.

Exeunt

V.2   *Drum and colours. Enter Menteth, Cathness, Angus,*
           Lennox, Soldiers

MENTETH

The English power is near, led on by Malcolm,
His uncle Seyward and the good Macduff.
Revenges burn in them; for their dear causes
Would to the bleeding and the grim alarm
Excite the mortified man.

ANGUS   Near Birnan Wood
Shall we well meet them; that way are they coming.

CATHNESS

Who knows if Donalbain be with his brother?

LENNOX

For certain, sir, he is not. I have a file
Of all the gentry: there is Seyward's son
10   And many unrough youths that even now
Protest their first of manhood.

MENTETH   What does the tyrant?

CATHNESS

Great Dunsinane he strongly fortifies.

Some say he's mad. Others, that lesser hate him,
Do call it valiant fury; but for certain
He cannot buckle his distempered cause
Within the belt of rule.

ANGUS   Now does he feel
His secret murders sticking on his hands;
Now minutely revolts upbraid his faith-breach.
Those he commands move only in command,
Nothing in love. Now does he feel his title   20
Hang loose about him like a giant's robe
Upon a dwarfish thief.

MENTETH   Who then shall blame
His pestered senses to recoil and start,
When all that is within him does condemn
Itself for being there?

CATHNESS   Well, march we on
To give obedience where 'tis truly owed.
Meet we the medicine of the sickly weal,
And with him pour we in our country's purge
Each drop of us.

LENNOX   Or so much as it needs
To dew the sovereign flower and drown the weeds.   30
Make we our march towards Birnan. *Exeunt, marching*

Enter Macbeth, Doctor, and Attendants   V.3
MACBETH
Bring me no more reports; let them fly all.
Till Birnan Wood remove to Dunsinane
I cannot taint with fear. What's the boy Malcolm?
Was he not born of woman? The spirits that know
All mortal consequences have pronounced me thus:
'Fear not, Macbeth; no man that's born of woman
Shall e'er have power upon thee.' Then fly, false thanes,

And mingle with the English epicures.
The mind I sway by and the heart I bear
10 Shall never sag with doubt nor shake with fear.

Enter Servant

The devil damn thee black, thou cream-faced loon!
Where got'st thou that goose look?

SERVANT
There is ten thousand –

MACBETH   Geese, villain?

SERVANT   Soldiers, sir.

MACBETH
Go prick thy face and over-red thy fear,
Thou lily-livered boy. What soldiers, patch?
Death of thy soul! Those linen cheeks of thine
Are counsellors to fear. What soldiers, whey-face?

SERVANT
The English force, so please you.

MACBETH
Take thy face hence.   *Exit Servant*
                    Seyton! – I am sick at heart
20 When I behold – Seyton, I say! – This push
Will chair me ever or dis-seat me now.
I have lived long enough: my way of life
Is fallen into the sere, the yellow leaf;
And that which should accompany old age,
As honour, love, obedience, troops of friends,
I must not look to have; but, in their stead,
Curses, not loud, but deep, mouth-honour, breath
Which the poor heart would fain deny and dare not. ·
Seyton!

Enter Seyton

SEYTON
What's your gracious pleasure?

30 MACBETH   What news more?

128

SEYTON

  All is confirmed, my lord, which was reported.

MACBETH

  I'll fight till from my bones my flesh be hacked.
  Give me my armour.

SEYTON   'Tis not needed yet.

MACBETH

  I'll put it on.
  Send out more horses, skirr the country round,
  Hang those that talk of fear. - Give me mine armour. -
  How does your patient, doctor?

DOCTOR   Not so sick, my lord,
  As she is troubled with thick-coming fancies
  That keep her from her rest.

MACBETH   Cure her of that.

  Canst thou not minister to a mind diseased,   40
  Pluck from the memory a rooted sorrow,
  Raze out the written troubles of the brain,
  And with some sweet oblivious antidote
  Cleanse the stuffed bosom of that perilous stuff
  Which weighs upon the heart?

DOCTOR   Therein the patient
  Must minister to himself.

MACBETH

  Throw physic to the dogs! I'll none of it. -
  Come, put mine armour on, give me my staff.
  Seyton, send out. - Doctor, the thanes fly from me. -
  Come, sir, dispatch. - If thou couldst, doctor, cast   50
  The water of my land, find her disease
  And purge it to a sound and pristine health,
  I would applaud thee to the very echo
  That should applaud again. - Pull't off, I say. -
  What rhubarb, senna, or what purgative drug
  Would scour these English hence? Hear'st thou of them?

DOCTOR

Ay, my good lord; your royal preparation
Makes us hear something.

MACBETH   — Bring it after me.

I will not be afraid of death and bane
60 Till Birnan forest come to Dunsinane.   *Exit*

DOCTOR

Were I from Dunsinane away and clear,
Profit again should hardly draw me here.   *Exit*

V.4   *Drum and colours. Enter Malcolm, Seyward, Mac-*
             duff, Seyward's Son, Menteth, Cathness, Angus, and
             Soldiers marching

MALCOLM

Cousins, I hope the days are near at hand
That chambers will be safe.

MENTETH   We doubt it nothing.

SEYWARD

What wood is this before us?

MENTETH   The wood of Birnan.

MALCOLM

Let every soldier hew him down a bough
And bear't before him; thereby shall we shadow
The numbers of our host and make discovery
Err in report of us.

SOLDIERS   It shall be done.

SEYWARD

We learn no other but the confident tyrant
Keeps still in Dunsinane and will endure
Our setting down before't.

10 MALCOLM   'Tis his main hope.

For where there is advantage to be given,
Both more and less have given him the revolt,

130

And none serve with him but constrainèd things
Whose hearts are absent too.

MACDUFF   Let our just censures
Attend the true event, and put we on
Industrious soldiership.

SEYWARD   The time approaches
That will with due decision make us know
What we shall say we have, and what we owe.
Thoughts speculative their unsure hopes relate,
But certain issue strokes must arbitrate;   20
Towards which, advance the war.   *Exeunt, marching*

Enter Macbeth, Seyton, and Soldiers, with drum and V.5
colours

MACBETH

Hang out our banners on the outward walls.
The cry is still, 'They come.' Our castle's strength
Will laugh a siege to scorn. Here let them lie
Till famine and the ague eat them up.
Were they not farced with those that should be ours
We might have met them dareful, beard to beard,
And beat them backward home.
    A cry within of women
                       What is that noise?

SEYTON

It is the cry of women, my good lord.   *Exit*

MACBETH

I have almost forgot the taste of fears.
The time has been my senses would have cooled   10
To hear a night-shriek, and my fell of hair
Would at a dismal treatise rouse and stir
As life were in't. I have supped full with horrors:
Direness, familiar to my slaughterous thoughts,

Cannot once start me.
>*Enter Seyton*

Wherefore was that cry?

SEYTON

The queen, my lord, is dead.

MACBETH

She should have died hereafter.
There would have been a time for such a word –
Tomorrow, and tomorrow, and tomorrow,
Creeps in this petty pace from day to day
To the last syllable of recorded time;
And all our yesterdays have lighted fools
The way to dusty death. Out, out, brief candle!
Life's but a walking shadow, a poor player
That struts and frets his hour upon the stage
And then is heard no more. It is a tale
Told by an idiot, full of sound and fury,
Signifying nothing.
>*Enter a Messenger*

Thou com'st to use thy tongue: thy story quickly!

MESSENGER

Gracious my lord,
I should report that which I say I saw,
But know not how to do't.

MACBETH   Well, say, sir.

MESSENGER

As I did stand my watch upon the hill
I looked toward Birnan and anon methought
The wood began to move.

MACBETH   Liar and slave!

MESSENGER

Let me endure your wrath if't be not so.
Within this three mile may you see it coming.
I say, a moving grove.

MACBETH   If thou speak'st false,
Upon the next tree shall thou hang alive
Till famine cling thee. If thy speech be sooth,   40
I care not if thou dost for me as much.
I pull in resolution, and begin
To doubt the equivocation of the fiend
That lies like truth. 'Fear not till Birnan Wood
Do come to Dunsinane' – and now a wood
Comes toward Dunsinane. Arm, arm, and out!
If this which he avouches does appear,
There is nor flying hence nor tarrying here.
I 'gin to be aweary of the sun,
And wish the estate o'the world were now undone. –   50
Ring the alarum bell! – Blow wind, come wrack,
At least we'll die with harness on our back.   *Exeunt*

V.6   *Drum and colours. Enter Malcolm, Seyward, Mac-
             duff, and their army, with boughs*

MALCOLM
Now near enough. Your leavy screens throw down,
And show like those you are. You, worthy uncle,
Shall with my cousin, your right noble son,
Lead our first battle. Worthy Macduff and we
Shall take upon's what else remains to do,
According to our order.
SEYWARD   Fare you well.
Do we but find the tyrant's power tonight,
Let us be beaten if we cannot fight.
MACDUFF
Make all our trumpets speak, give them all breath,
Those clamorous harbingers of blood and death.   10
                                                Exeunt

     Alarums continued

Enter Macbeth

MACBETH
   They have tied me to a stake, I cannot fly,
   But bear-like I must fight the course. What's he
   That was not born of woman? Such a one
   Am I to fear, or none.
      Enter Young Seyward

YOUNG SEYWARD
   What is thy name?

MACBETH   Thou'lt be afraid to hear it.

YOUNG SEYWARD
   No, though thou call'st thyself a hotter name
   Than any is in hell.

MACBETH   My name's Macbeth.

YOUNG SEYWARD
   The devil himself could not pronounce a title
   More hateful to mine ear.

MACBETH   No, nor more fearful.

YOUNG SEYWARD
60   Thou liest, abhorrèd tyrant! With my sword
   I'll prove the lie thou speak'st.
      Fight, and Young Seyward slain

MACBETH   Thou wast born of woman.
   But swords I smile at, weapons laugh to scorn,
   Brandished by man that's of a woman born.   *Exit*
      Alarums. Enter Macduff

MACDUFF
   That way the noise is. Tyrant, show thy face.
   If thou be'st slain, and with no stroke of mine,
   My wife and children's ghosts will haunt me still.
   I cannot strike at wretched kerns, whose arms
   Are hired to bear their staves. Either thou, Macbeth,
   Or else my sword with an unbattered edge
70   I sheathe again undeeded. There thou shouldst be:

By this great clatter one of greatest note
Seems bruited. Let me find him, fortune!
And more I beg not.   *Exit*
    Alarums. Enter Malcolm and Seyward

SEYWARD

This way, my lord. The castle's gently rendered.
The tyrant's people on both sides do fight;
The noble thanes do bravely in the war;
The day almost itself professes yours,
And little is to do.

MALCOLM   We have met with foes
That strike beside us.

SEYWARD   Enter, sir, the castle.   *Exeunt*
    Alarum. Enter Macbeth

MACBETH

Why should I play the Roman fool and die   40
On mine own sword? Whiles I see lives, the gashes
Do better upon them.
    Enter Macduff

MACDUFF   Turn, hellhound, turn!

MACBETH

Of all men else I have avoided thee.
But get thee back; my soul is too much charged
With blood of thine already.

MACDUFF   I have no words;
My voice is in my sword, thou bloodier villain
Than terms can give thee out.
    Fight. Alarum

MACBETH   Thou losest labour.
As easy mayst thou the intrenchant air
With thy keen sword impress, as make me bleed.
Let fall thy blade on vulnerable crests,   50
I bear a charmèd life which must not yield
To one of woman born.

MACDUFF   Despair thy charm,
And let the angel whom thou still hast served
Tell thee Macduff was from his mother's womb
Untimely ripped.

MACBETH
Accursèd be that tongue that tells me so;
For it hath cowed my better part of man;
And be these juggling fiends no more believed
That palter with us in a double sense,
60   That keep the word of promise to our ear
And break it to our hope. I'll not fight with thee.

MACDUFF
Then yield thee, coward;
And live to be the show and gaze o'the time.
We'll have thee, as our rarer monsters are,
Painted upon a pole, and underwrit,
'Here may you see the tyrant.'

MACBETH   I will not yield
To kiss the ground before young Malcolm's feet
And to be baited with the rabble's curse.
Though Birnan Wood be come to Dunsinane
70   And thou opposed, being of no woman born,
Yet I will try the last. Before my body
I throw my warlike shield. Lay on, Macduff;
And damned be him that first cries, 'Hold, enough!'

                                            Exeunt fighting
        Alarums. Enter fighting. and Macbeth slain
                                            Exit Macduff
        Retreat and flourish. Enter with drum and colours
        Malcolm, Seyward, Ross, Thanes, and Soldiers

MALCOLM
I would the friends we miss were safe arrived.

SEYWARD
Some must go off; and yet, by these I see

So great a day as this is cheaply bought.

MALCOLM

Macduff is missing and your noble son.

ROSS

Your son, my lord, has paid a soldier's debt.
He only lived but till he was a man;
The which no sooner had his prowess confirmed   80
In the unshrinking station where he fought
But, like a man, he died.

SEYWARD   Then he is dead?

ROSS

Ay, and brought off the field. Your cause of sorrow
Must not be measured by his worth, for then
It hath no end.

SEYWARD   Had he his hurts before?

ROSS

Ay, on the front.

SEYWARD   Why then, God's soldier be he.
Had I as many sons as I have hairs
I would not wish them to a fairer death.
And so his knell is knolled.

MALCOLM   He's worth more sorrow;
And that I'll spend for him.

SEYWARD   He's worth no more: 90
They say he parted well, and paid his score.
And so God be with him. – Here comes newer comfort.

Enter Macduff with Macbeth's head

MACDUFF

Hail, King! For so thou art. Behold where stands
The usurper's cursèd head. The time is free.
I see thee compassed with thy kingdom's pearl
That speak my salutation in their minds,
Whose voices I desire aloud with mine. –
Hail, King of Scotland!

ALL   Hail, King of Scotland!

Flourish

MALCOLM

 We shall not spend a large expense of time
100 Before we reckon with your several loves,
 And make us even with you. My thanes and kinsmen,
 Henceforth be earls, the first that ever Scotland
 In such an honour named. What's more to do,
 Which would be planted newly with the time,
 As calling home our exiled friends abroad
 That fled the snares of watchful tyranny,
 Producing forth the cruel ministers
 Of this dead butcher and his fiend-like queen –
 Who, as 'tis thought, by self and violent hands
110 Took off her life – this, and what needful else
 That calls upon us, by the grace of Grace
 We will perform in measure, time, and place.
 So thanks to all at once, and to each one,
 Whom we invite to see us crowned at Scone.

         Flourish. Exeunt

COMMENTARY

'F' below, and in the Account of the Text, refers to the text contained in the first Folio of Shakespeare's works (1623).

I.1   'The true reason for the first appearance of the witches is to strike the keynote of the character of the whole drama' (Coleridge).

3   *hurly-burly* confused turmoil

4   *lost and won.* This is purposefully equivocal. When 'Fair is foul' (line 9), losing may count as winning.

8   *Grey-Malkin, Padock.* These are the 'familiars' or demon-companions of the witches. The usual identification of the first and second familiars with a cat and a toad is not fully confirmed by IV.1.1–3, and must be left undecided.

    Anon soon. The Third Witch replies to her (unnamed) familiar.

10   *Hover.* This may be taken to imply that the witches depart by flying.

I.2   The bleeding sergeant – himself an effective symbol of the battle he describes, and of Macbeth's part therein – speaks the inflated language suitable to his function as a passionate and weighty messenger. The *Alarum* at the beginning of the scene should form a natural bridge between the 'filthy air' of the witches' exit and the blood-daubed human being who staggers in from their 'hurly-burly'.

3   *sergeant* (a word of three syllables). The rank is not that

139

of the modern N.C.O. but of an officer who is called 'Captain' in the stage direction.

9	*choke their art* make impossible the art of swimming
10	*to that* as if to that end
11-12	*multiplying villainies of nature	Do swarm upon him* hosts of rebels join him like noxious insects swarming
12	*Western Isles* Hebrides
13	*kerns and galloglasses* light and heavy-armed Celtic levies
16	*that name* (brave)
20	*the slave* Macdonwald
21	*ne'er shook hands nor bade farewell to him* engaged in none of the courtesies (or decencies) of war
22	*nave to the chops* navel to the jaws
24	*cousin.* This is a general term of kinship; but accurate (in the modern sense) here.
25	*reflection* turning-back at the vernal equinox
26	*thunders.* The rhythm of the line is very often pieced-out by adding a verb ('break' is the favourite). But both rhythm and syntax work by suspension; the discord is not resolved till we reach *come* in the following line.
30	*skipping* lightly armed (perhaps also with the sense of 'foot-loose', 'light in allegiance')
31	*Norweyan.* The sources say 'Danish'. It has been suggested that Shakespeare changed this to avoid giving offence to Christian IV. See Introduction, p. 29.
	surveying vantage seeing his chance
36	*say sooth* tell the truth
38	*So they.* This short line, in the manner of Virgil, is used (like the epic simile) to mark the heroic technique of the messenger's speech.
41	*memorize another Golgotha* make another field of the dead as memorable as Calvary
48	*seems to* shows he is going to
53	*Norway* the King of Norway
56	*Bellona's bridegroom* (Macbeth, fit husband for the goddess of war)

56   *lapped in proof* clad in tested armour

57   *him* the King of Norway

       self-comparisons (1) in terms of bravery; (2) (ironically) in terms of treason

58   *Point against point-rebellious, arm* ... F reads 'Point, rebellious'; most editors suppose that this makes *rebellious* qualify *arm*. I take the comma to be here (as often) equivalent to the modern hyphen, so that the first phrase means 'sword raised against rebellious sword'.

59   *lavish* excessive, ill-disciplined

62   *composition* truce, agreement

64   *Saint Colm's Inch* Inchcolm (in the Firth of Forth)

70   *What he hath lost, noble Macbeth hath won.* Note the ironic assimilation of the past traitor, Cawdor, and the future traitor, Macbeth.

I.3   This climatic scene brings together the thesis and antithesis of the first two scenes – the withered sisters and the blood-soaked soldiers. It reveals the quality of Macbeth's nature and contrasts that of Banquo; but it leaves the future open and ambiguous.

2   *Killing swine* (the bloodiest of domestic slaughterings)

6   *Aroint thee* begone

       ronyon (term of abuse)

7   *Tiger.* This was an actual ship that sailed to Aleppo in 1583; it was in the London news in 1606. It sailed from England on 5 December 1604 and arrived back after fearful experiences on 27 June 1606. If we call the time away 568 days, this would be close enough to the 'Weary sev'n-nights nine times nine' that the witches calculate (567 days).

9   *without a tail.* Impersonation by witchcraft was liable to deficiencies of this kind.

10   *do* (as in the modern vague abusive 'I'll do him' = 'I'll cause him harm')

15 *the very ports they blow*. The winds blow *from* the ports, so that it is impossible to enter them.

16 *quarters* directions

17 *card* compass

18-23 *I'll drain him dry as hay . . . peak, and pine.* Though ostensibly about the master of the *Tiger*, this serves as an accurate forecast of the fate of Macbeth. But lines 24-5 indicate an alternative ending to the story.

20 *penthouse* a lean-to shed (his eyelids, oppressed by sleep, will slope over his eyes like the roof of a penthouse)

23 *peak* grow thin and sharp-featured

31 *Weird Sisters. Wyrd* is the Anglo-Saxon word for fate and *Weird* (noun) is the medieval and (later) northern form for one of the three Fates or Destinies – sometimes called the *Weird Sisters*. This was the nomenclature that Shakespeare inherited, but subsequent use of the phrase has been largely affected by *Macbeth*. The F spelling *weyard* gives a necessary clue to Shakespeare's pronunciation.

32 *Posters* travellers

37 *So foul and fair a day* (catching up the 'Fair is foul' exit of the witches in I.1; so that, on entering, Macbeth seems to be entering into *their* world, in mind as well as body)

38 *is't called* is it said to be; is it

43 *choppy* chapped, and so rough. The Witches lay their fingers to their lips, presumably to indicate the secret or forbidden nature of their communication.

47-9 *All hail.* It is worth noticing that Shakespeare elsewhere (*Richard II*, IV.1.169) associates this phrase with Judas's betrayal of Christ.

47 *Glamis.* It appears (I.5.13 and elsewhere) that Shakespeare used a two-syllable pronunciation of this word, 'Gla-miss', rather than the modern 'Glams'.

50-51 Note the pun on *fear* and *fair* (pronounced alike in Shakespeare's day).

52 *fantastical* imaginary

69 *imperfect* insufficiently explicit

70 *Sinell* (a name for Macbeth's father)

71 *The Thane of Cawdor lives.* Evidently Macbeth does not know that the Thane of Cawdor has been assisting Norway.

83 *the insane root* any root that makes insane those who eat it

91–2 *His wonders and his praises do contend | Which should be thine, or his.* If he expresses his wonder (is dumbfounded) he cannot convey your praises. If he praises you he cannot express his own wonder (by being dumb)

103 *earnest* pledge
  a greater honour. Presumably Ross is only trying to convey Duncan's hyperbolic promises. But Macbeth (and the audience) are bound to think of the third prophecy.

111 *line* support
  rebel Macdonwald

119 *home* all the way

127 *swelling Act* magnificent theatrical experience

129 *soliciting* allurement. (This is not really true; the witches do not allure; they simply present; but Macbeth's mind sees their words as allurement.)

130 *Cannot be ill, cannot be good* (a subjective equivalent to 'Fair is foul')

133 *suggestion* prompting or incitement to evil

134 *horrid* literally 'bristling' (like the *hair*)

136–7 *Present fears | Are less than horrible imaginings.* Frightful things in the present have less effect on us than imagined horrors.

138 *fantastical* imaginary

139 *single* individual (sometimes taken to mean 'weak')

140–41 *function is smothered in surmise, | And nothing is but what is not* the power to act is annihilated by my speculations; so that the only thing that exists in the present is what does not really exist in the present – thoughts of the future

146 *Come what come may* whatever happens

147 *Time and the hour runs through the roughest day.* Whatever is going to happen *will* happen, inevitably.

149-50 *My dull brain was wrought | With things forgotten.* Macbeth excuses his inattention by the lie that his mind is caught up in things of the past. In fact, it is caught up in the future.

155 *free hearts* open feelings

I.4 The first Cawdor's good end is played against the second Cawdor's bad beginning. The court of Duncan is revealed as a family unit, bound by natural ties of trust and loyalty. The naming of the heir, which might have given the historical Macbeth a legitimate cause to supplant the King, is here brought forward without this political consequence; it merely isolates Macbeth from the national life, drives him further into the world of his imagination.

10 *had been studied* had learned his part in the play

11 *owed* owned

15 *O worthiest cousin!* Note the ironic turn from Cawdor, as a traitorous hypocrite, to Macbeth.

17 *before* in advance of my power of repayment

20 *proportion both of thanks and payment* the weighing up how much was due and how much should be paid

21-2 *Only I have left to say, | 'More is thy due than more than all can pay'* all that I have to pay you with is the statement that I cannot repay you

23-4 *The service and the loyalty I owe, | In doing it, pays itself* the reward for service and loyalty is found in the joy of doing loyal acts of service

25-8 *and our duties ... to your throne ... do but what they should by doing everything | Safe toward your love and honour* our duties to your throne only express their nature as absolute dependants when they are doing everything possible to protect you

37   *you whose places are the nearest* the next nearest to the throne (after the *Sons, kinsmen, thanes*)

38   *estate* state, kingdom

45   *The rest is labour, which is not used for you* it is wearisome to be inactive, when we know we ought to be doing something to serve you

46   *harbinger* officer sent ahead of the king to arrange his lodgings

53   *wink* keep shut

     let that be may the action come into being

I.5   The violent certainty of Lady Macbeth acts as a catalyst to crystallize a mode of action and of character-development out of the uncertainties of previous scenes. At the same time a new and more intimate image of Macbeth emerges to complicate what we have known and guessed at.

15   *human-kindness* the quality of creatureliness, or humanity, that he sucked from his mother; what binds the individual to the social order of Man. (There is no evidence that Lady Macbeth has to fear the *kindness* – in the ordinary modern sense – of Macbeth's nature.)

18   *illness* wickedness

     highly greatly

21   *That which cries, 'Thus thou must do' if thou have it.* The ambitious ends proposed cry out for immoral action on the part of anyone who hopes to achieve them.

22   *that* (the end which Macbeth 'wouldst . . . have')

24   *That I may pour my spirits in thine ear* (as Claudius poisoned the elder Hamlet)

27   *metaphysical* supernatural

35   *tending* attendance

36   *raven* (messenger of death)

37   *fatal* (to Duncan)

39   *mortal thoughts* murderous designs

     unsex take away my feminine qualities

41   *Make thick my blood* ('so that pity cannot flow along her veins and reach her heart' – Bradley)

44–5   *keep peace between | The effect and it* act as a restraining influence, and so impede the translation of purpose into effect

46   *take my milk for gall* 'take away my milk and put gall into the place' (Dr Johnson)

     murdering ministers agents of murder (the 'spirits' of line 38)

47   *sightless* invisible

48   *wait on nature's mischief* accompany natural disasters

49   *pall thee* wrap yourself

53   *the all-hail hereafter.* The third 'All hail' with which the Witches greeted Macbeth (I.3.49) prophesied that he should become King. Lady Macbeth refers to this future state.

61–2   *To beguile the time | Look like the time* to deceive people look as they expect you to look

70   *favour* face, appearance

I.6   The final calm before the storm. In immediate contrast to the enclosed darkness of the previous scene is the open, light naturalness of this one. The elaboration of Lady Macbeth's rhetoric is a symptom of her falsity. (stage direction) *Hautboys and torches.* Are these needed in this daylight scene? Perhaps the attendants who normally perform these functions are meant.

1   *seat* situation

1–3   *the air | Nimbly and sweetly recommends itself | Unto our gentle senses* the air is prompt to come forward and show its merits

3   *gentle senses* (perhaps 'the senses which the air greets like gentlemen' or simply 'our refined sensibilities')

4 *temple-haunting martlet* the martin, commonly building its nest in churches

   approve prove

5 *his loved mansionry* his love of building here

6 *jutty* projection

7 *coign of vantage* advantageous corner

9 *haunt* frequent

11-14 *The love that follows us sometime is our trouble, | Which still we thank as love. Herein I teach you | How you shall bid 'God 'ield us' for your pains, | And thank us for your trouble* I have followed you to Inverness. This indicates my love; yet it is also troublesome. However in such situations we tend to think of the love and ignore the trouble. By saying this I have taught you how to pray for the good of those who trouble you

13 *bid* pray

16 *single* slight, trivial

20 *We rest your hermits* we remain bound to pray for you

22 *purveyor* officer sent in advance, to obtain food for the main party

26-8 *in compt, | To make their audit at your highness' pleasure, | Still to return your own.* Macbeth and his Lady are only the *stewards* of their possessions; they are ready to account for them and render them up whenever Duncan, the real owner, requires.

I.7 This scene is the climax of Act I, with the order and the disorder themes brought into sharpest opposition. The opening dumb-show of feasting must create a context of trust and benevolence around Macbeth's soliloquy and the dialogue that follows, so as to keep the argument for society before our eyes while (with our minds) we see the individual move towards his great betrayal.

   (stage direction) *Sewer* superintendent of the feast

1   *If it were done when 'tis done* if the doing of the deed were the end of it

3   *trammel up the consequence* catch up (as in a net) the trail of consequences that follows any action. (The metaphor is continued in *catch | With his surcease success*.)

4   *With his surcease.* Either (1) by Duncan's death or (2) by putting an end to the consequences. Shakespeare regularly uses *his* for modern 'its'.
        that but so that only

6   *bank and shoal.* The F 'Banke and Schoole' can be seen simply as an older spelling of the version printed here - the sense being that time is only an isthmus between two eternities. On the other hand, *bank* often means *bench*, and the train of words 'bank . . . school . . . judgement . . . teach' seems significant.

7   *jump the life to come* hazard things outside the scope of here-and-now

8   *that* in that

10   *even-handed justice* precise retribution. The lines which follow forecast the exact nature of Macbeth's fate - by destroying trust he destroys his own capacity for trust.

11   *ingredience* composition
        poisoned chalice. The chalice is a particularly treacherous vehicle of murder, being (like Macbeth's castle) the vessel of sacredness and trust.

17   *faculties* powers

18   *clear* spotless

22   *Striding the blast* astride the storm (of indignation)

22-3   *heaven's cherubin, horsed | Upon the sightless curriers of the air.* Probably suggested by the 18th Psalm: 'He rid upon the Cherub [A.V. *Cherubins*] and he did fly; he came fleeing upon the wings of the wind.' The *sightless* (invisible) *curriers* (runners) are the winds in motion. The baby Pity, and the baby-like cherubin (Shakespearian form of Hebrew *Cherubim*), will ride on the winds and blow the deed like dust into every eye, so that everyone will know it, and weep (1) because of the dust; (2) because of pity.

148

23   *curriers.* I have preserved this form (1) to avoid the inappropriate connotations of the modern *courier*; (2) to keep the short vowel-sound of the Elizabethan form, in a line requiring (because of the sense) to be made up of short sounds. F reads 'Curriors'.

25   *That tears shall drown the wind* ('alluding to the remission of the wind in a shower' - Johnson)

25–8   *I have no spur | To prick the sides of my intent but only | Vaulting ambition which o'erleaps itself | And falls on the other.* The horse imagery of 'Striding' and 'horsed' leads now (1) to a view of Macbeth's intention to murder as a horse that must be spurred, and (2) to a view of ambition (which could be a spur or stimulus) as a rider vaulting into his saddle, but overshooting the mark and falling on the other side.

28   *the other* (side)
       (stage direction) *Enter Lady Macbeth* (sometimes seen as an ironic answer to Macbeth's *I have no spur*)

32   *bought* (by his bravery in battle)

34   *in their newest gloss.* The 'Golden opinions' are seen as new suits of clothes.

37   *green and pale* nauseated, as in the morning after drunkenness

39   *Such* (as drunken lechery)

41–2   *that | Which thou esteem'st the ornament of life* (greatness, the crown)

44   *wait upon* accompany

45   *the adage* (the proverb: 'the cat wanted to eat fish, but would not wet her feet')

46–7   *I dare do all that may become a man; | Who dares do more is none* to be daring is manly; but to be too daring may carry one right outside the limits proper to human (and humane) activity. Lady Macbeth's reply is that a man deficient in continued daring is a *beast*. To exceed in daring is to exceed in *manliness*. She chooses to ignore the question of *humanity*

48   *break this enterprise to me.* Presumably she refers to the letter she reads above, so that what she says is not

literally true; but Lady Macbeth is persuading, not recounting, and neither she nor Shakespeare is bound to literal truth.

53   *They have made themselves* (Duncan is now in our power) *that their fitness* that fitness of theirs (fitness of time and place for the murder)

54   *unmake you* make you incapable

59–61   *We fail! | But screw your courage to the sticking place, | And we'll not fail.* Lady Macbeth's reply is printed in F as a question – but the question-mark then served also for the exclamation-mark. If she scornfully repeats Macbeth's question, then *But* must mean 'only'. If (with an exclamation-mark) she accepts the possibility of failure, *But* is the usual disjunctive. I have preferred the latter interpretation.

60   *screw your courage to the sticking place.* The metaphor is from the cross-bow, in which the 'sticking place' was the notch into which the string fitted when sufficiently 'screwed up'.

63   *chamberlains* attendants on the bed-chamber

64   *wassail* festivity
     convince overcome

65   *the warder of the brain* (memory guards us against the performance of deeds that proved shameful in the past)

66–7   *receipt of reason | A limbeck only.* The part of the brain where reasons are received or collected will be a retort or alembic, full of the fumes that accompany distillation.

68   *drenchèd* (with drink)

71   *spongy officers* (the drink-sodden chamberlains)

72   *quell* murder

72–4   *Bring forth men-children only! | For thy undaunted mettle should compose | Nothing but males.* Macbeth accepts and endorses his wife's version of 'manliness'.

74   *received* (by the minds of observers)

79–80   *bend up | Each corporal agent* strain every muscle

81   *mock the time.* Macbeth repeats his wife's advice to 'beguile the time' (I.5.61).

II.1 Just before the fatal deed Banquo is reintroduced beside Macbeth to highlight the central distinction
between a moral will and a moralizing imagination.

4 *husbandry* thrift (the heavens are *husbanding* their
resources)

5 *Take thee that too*. 'That is precisely what the actor who
plays Banquo hands to the actor (or actress) who plays
Fleance – "his dagger" in Booth's production; "his hat"
in Phelps's' (Sprague).

14 *offices* servants' quarters

16 *shut up* concluded his speech

18 *Our will became the servant to defect* our desire (to be
hospitable) was bound in by the limitations imposed by
our unpreparedness

25 *cleave to my consent when 'tis* adhere to my opinion when
we discuss the matter

27–8 *keep | My bosom franchised and allegiance clear* keep my
heart free from evil, and my allegiance to the King un-
tainted

36 *fatal* ominous
sensible open to sensory apprehension

42 *Thou marshall'st me the way that I was going.* The
visionary dagger seems to float before him and lead him
(like a *marshal* or usher) to the door of Duncan's bed-
chamber.

44–5 *Mine eyes are made the fools o'th'other senses, | Or else
worth all the rest.* Either the dagger does not exist, in
which case the sight of it is false; or else the vision is of
a higher truth than that of normal sense-experience.

46 *dudgeon* handle
gouts drops

48 *informs* makes shapes

49 *half-world* hemisphere

51 *curtained* (1) behind bed-curtains; (2) hidden from
conscious control

51–2 *Witchcraft celebrates | Pale Hecat's offerings.* Witchcraft
celebrates its sacrificial rites to Hecat (goddess of

the moon as well as of witches, and therefore 'Pale').

53   *Alarumed* aroused

55   *Tarquin's ravishing strides* the stealthy steps that Tarquin took while moving towards his rape of Lucrece

58   *Thy very stones prate of my whereabout.* This is probably from Luke 19.40: 'if these hold their peace, then shall the stones cry'.

59   *take the present horror from the time* break the ghastly silence

II.2   An ecstasy of moral hysteria follows the murder. The disjointed language suggests both guilt and terror, in a kind of hell cut off from humanity, till reawakened by the 'knocking' at the end of the scene.

2   *quenched* made unconscious (by drink)

3   *fatal bellman.* The owl, as the bird of death, is compared to the bellman sent to give 'stern'st good-night' to condemned prisoners the night before their execution.

5   *The doors are open* (1) the physical impediments have been overcome; (2) moral restraints have been abolished

    grooms royal servants with specific household duties

6   *mock their charge* make a mockery of their duty to guard the King

    possets restorative night-drinks

7   *nature* the forces of life

13   *My husband* (the only time she uses this term throughout the play)

20   *sorry sight.* We heard much about the loyally bloodstained Macbeth in I.2. The first time we *see* him bloodstained it is with the blood of his rightful King.

21   *A foolish thought, to say a sorry sight.* Lady Macbeth attempts a comforting jocularity: 'It would be foolish (or "sorry") of you to feel sorrow for such a deed.'

22   *one did laugh in's sleep, and one cried 'Murder!'* Presumably Donalbain and his companion (Malcolm?) in

the second chamber (also the *one* and *other* of line 26).

27   *hangman's* bloody (because he dismembered as well as hanged)

30   *Consider* contemplate

32   *most need of blessing* (because he was falling into sin). Notice the avoidance of responsibility for his action.

34   *so* if you do so

37   *ravelled sleave* tangled skein

38   *bath* (that which eases the hurt)

39   *second course* (1) the most sustaining dish in the feast – the 'Chief nourisher' (anciently, meat came in the second course); (2) the second mode of existence

45   *unbend* dismantle

47   *filthy witness* (the tell-tale blood)

54-5   *pictures ... bleed.* Notice the stark contrast between these words. Lady Macbeth must be seen to be falsifying.

56-7   *I'll gild the faces of the grooms withal,* | *For it must seem their guilt.* The pun marks the tension of the moment: moreover, to Lady Macbeth '*guilt* is something like *gilt* – one can wash it off or paint it on' (Cleanth Brooks).

62   *multitudinous* 'multiform'; or 'teeming with multitudes of creatures'
         incarnadine turn red

63   *green one red* either 'green-one red' or 'green, one red'. Compare Revelation 16.3: 'And the second angel shed his vial upon the sea, and it turned as it were into the blood of a dead man.'

64   *My hands are of your colour* (from 'gilding' the faces of the chamberlains)

67   *A little water* (in strong contrast to *multitudinous seas* above)

71   *watchers* awake (*watch* is a variant form of 'wake')

73   *To know my deed 'twere best not know myself.* If I am to think about the murder I must stop being conscious of the man I have been.

II.3   This scene is sometimes thought un-Shakespearian because 'low'. But the Porter scene is a typically Elizabethan 'double-take' of damnation and its precedents, based on the tradition of 'Estates-Satire', in which 'some of all professions' (line 17) were surveyed and condemned. The Porter of hell-gate was a figure in the medieval drama, an opposite to St Peter, and opponent of Christ in 'the harrowing of Hell'. The faked business of the following 'council scene' (undercut by the asides of Malcolm and Donalbain) points forward to the emptiness of social gatherings under Macbeth.

    (stage direction) *within* behind the stage façade (meaning *outside* in terms of stage illusion)

2   *old* plenty of (colloquial intensive)

4-5   *Here's a farmer that hanged himself on the expectation of plenty.* The farmer stored his crops, hoping that prices would rise; when the next season produced an expectation of plentiful crops, prices fell and he hanged himself (the traditional expression of religious despair).

5   *Come in time.* This, the F reading, makes a weak kind of sense: 'Come in good time.' Dover Wilson's emendation to 'time-server' is attractive and apposite, but not necessary.

    napkins (to mop up the sweat. Did the farmer hang himself in his napkin?)

7   *the other devil.* The Porter wishes to mention some devil other than Belzebub (line 4), but cannot remember the name of any.

8   *equivocator.* Usually taken as a reference to the Jesuits, and especially to Father Garnet who, in the Gunpowder Plot trial, 'equivocated', swore evidence with mental reservation that it was not true. But equivocation (by Witches, by Macbeth) runs throughout the whole play. See Introduction (p. 40).

9-10   *treason enough for God's sake* (presumably another reference to the Jesuit)

13-14   *stealing out of a French hose.* 'Hose' were breeches, which about the time of *Macbeth* changed fashion from wide to narrow ('French') fitting. The tailor had been accustomed to steal cloth from the baggy breeches, but was detected in the closer-fitting ones.

14   *roast your goose* (1) heat your smoothing iron (goose); (2) ? 'cook your goose' (undo yourself)

19   *I pray you remember the porter*. Returning to his role as the company clown, the Porter begs for a tip.

22–3   *second cock* three o'clock in the morning. (It is now daybreak.)

32–3   *equivocates him in a sleep* fulfils his lechery only in a dream

33   *giving him the lie* (1) deceives him; (2) floors him; (3) makes him urinate (lie=lye)

37   *took up my legs* (as a wrestler lifts his opponent)

38   *cast* (1) throw (as in wrestling); (2) vomit

43   *timely* early

47   *The labour we delight in physics pain* when we enjoy doing something, the enjoyment counters the laboriousness

49   *limited* appointed

52–6   *Our chimneys were blown down . . . woeful time*. Nature expresses the breach of natural order by 'natural' convulsions.

56   *New-hatched to the woeful time* newly emerged to make the time woeful

       obscure bird (the owl, bird of darkness, thought to portend death)

61   *Tongue nor heart cannot conceive nor name thee!* Note the chiastic order: it is the heart which conceives, the tongue which names.

63   *Confusion* destruction

65   *The Lord's anointed temple* the temple (body) of the Lord's anointed (combining 2 Corinthians 6.16: 'Ye [Christians] are the temple of the living God' and I Samuel 24.10: 'the Lord's anointed'. Note the context of this latter passage)

69   *Gorgon*. She turned to stone those who looked on her.

75   *Great Doom's image* a replica of the Last Judgement

76   *As from your graves rise up* act as if at the Last Judge-
      ment itself, to fit in with the present horror ('coun-
      tenance' is also used in the sense of 'behold')

77   *Ring the bell!* This is sometimes supposed to be a stage
      direction added by the prompter, and accidentally
      printed as part of the text.

79   *trumpet.* The trumpet is an appropriate metaphor for
      the bell, because of the Last Judgement atmosphere.

90   *mortality* human life

92   *lees* dregs

93   *vault* (1) wine vault; (2) sky

94   *You are* (you are amiss, since you have lost your father)

99   *badged* marked

107   *expedition* haste

108   *pauser* that should make one pause

109   *His silver skin laced with his golden blood* ('dressed in the
      most precious of garments, the royal blood itself' –
      Cleanth Brooks)

113   *Unmannerly breeched* wearing an improper (? inhuman)
      kind of breeches (the blood of the King, the man they
      should defend)

115   (stage direction) *swooning.* Critics dispute whether this
      is a genuine swoon (due to womanly exhaustion) or a
      ruse (designed to distract attention from her husband).

117   *argument* theme of discourse (here, the horror of Dun-
      can's death)

119   *Hid in an auger-hole* concealed, by treachery, in the
      smallest crevice

120   *brewed* matured

121   *strong sorrow upon the foot of motion.* Our sorrow is
      stronger than shows at the moment; it has not yet begun
      to move, to take action.

123   *our naked frailties hid* clothed our poor, half-naked
      bodies – with a side-glance at the frailty of the whole
      human condition

126   *scruples* doubts

127   *In the great hand of God I stand* I put myself at God's disposal (to be compared with Macbeth's appeal for '*manly* readiness' below)
           thence relying on God

128   *undivulged pretence* purpose as yet unrevealed

130   *put on manly readiness* put on clothes *and* resolute minds

137-8   *The nea'er in blood | The nearer bloody* the more closely related people are, the more likely they are to try to murder us

140   *the aim* the beginning of the purpose

141   *dainty of* particular about

142-3   *There's warrant in that theft | Which steals itself when there's no mercy left* in these circumstances to steal away is a justified kind of stealing

II.4   This scene serves to slow down the time movement and to withdraw the camera from the agonizing close-ups of the preceding episodes. The Old Man here is a choric figure, imported to give a view of the action from outside, and to show it in large-scale perspective. The natural 'portents' take their place in this perspective as expressing heaven's view of what has happened.

4   *trifled* made trivial
           father old man

5-6   *heavens . . . act . . . stage* (all theatrical terms)

7   *travelling lamp* the sun

12   *towering in her pride of place* circling to reach her highest pitch (technical terms of falconry)

13   *a mousing owl* (an owl whose nature it is to hunt close to the ground for mice, not for falcons)

15   *minions of their race* the darlings of horse-breeding

24   *pretend* intend
           suborned bribed to do evil

28-9   *raven up | Thine own life's means* devour improvidently the sustenance (lineal respect, paternal love) on which their life and their own succession depended

30   *sovereignty will fall upon Macbeth.* Macbeth was the
       next heir, Duncan and Macbeth both being grandsons,
       of the older and younger branches respectively, of
       Malcolm II, the previous king.

33   *Colmekill* Iona (the burial-place of Scottish kings from
       973 to 1040)

36   *Fife* (Macduff's own territory)

38   *Lest our old robes sit easier than our new* (the new
       monarch is likely to be more severe than the former one)

40-41 *God's benison go with you, and with those | That would
       make good of bad, and friends of foes!* Blessed be the
       peacemakers.

III.1   After some time has elapsed we meet Macbeth again
        and note that he has developed into a very poised tyrant.
        The contrast with Banquo is one which he cannot now
        bear, and his new skill is shown in his organizing the
        means to remove his 'enemy'.

4   *stand in thy posterity* remain in your family

7   *shine* are glowingly fulfilled

10   (stage direction) *Sennet* flourish of trumpets to an-
       nounce important entry

15   *I'll* (condescension from the royal *we* to the personal *I*
       to indicate special affability - shown also by *request*)

16   *to the which.* The antecedent to *which* is the idea of 'your
       commandment'.

17   *indissoluble* (main stress on second syllable)

21   *still* always

25   *the better* better than that

32   *strange invention* (that Macbeth was the murderer)

33   *therewithal* besides that
       cause of state state business

42-3   *To make society the sweeter welcome, | We will keep our-
       self till supper-time alone* I will avoid company now so
       that it may be more pleasant when we meet again at
       supper

47   *To be thus* to be King

48–9   *Our fears in Banquo | Stick deep* our fear of Banquo is like a thorn in our flesh

49   *royalty of nature* natural regality of temper

50   *that* the 'royalty', a quality loftily independent of Macbeth's interests. Compare Iago's 'He hath a daily beauty in his life | That makes me ugly' in *Othello*, V.1.19–20.

55   *genius* guardian spirit
        it is said (by Plutarch, in the *Life of Antony*). Compare *Antony and Cleopatra*, II.3.29–31: 'thy spirit | Is all afraid to govern thee near him; | But, he away, 'tis noble.'

61   *grip.* Editors usually print 'gripe', the F form. But there seems no case against modernizing; in this sense, the two forms of the word are indistinguishable.

62   *unlineal* not of my family

64   *filed* defiled

65   *gracious* filled with (religious) grace

66   *Put rancours in the vessel of my peace* put irritants where there used to be peace. In view of the prevailingly religious tone of the context *vessel* may be the chalice and the whole phrase mean 'took me out of the state of grace'.

67   *eternal jewel* immortal soul

68   *the common enemy of man* the devil

70–71   *come fate into the list | And champion me to the utterance!* Let fate enter the tournament and face me in a duel *à outrance*, that is, to the death

76–7   *held you | So under fortune* kept you in a lowly condition

79   *passed in probation* went over the proofs

80   *borne in hand* kept in delusion
        instruments agents

82   *half a soul* a halfwit

83   *Banquo.* Notice how this essential information about the name of the person being discussed is delayed to the end of the speech.

87 *so gospelled* so meekly Christian (as to 'love your enemies, . . . pray for them which hurt you and persecute you' – Matthew 5.44)

90 *yours* (your family, your issue)

91-107 *Ay, in the catalogue ye go for men.* . . . Macbeth now uses the taunt of unmanliness which was so effective when used against him.

91 *catalogue* an undiscriminating list (set in contrast to the *valued file*)

93 *Shoughs* shaggy Icelandic dogs (probably pronounced to rhyme with *lochs*)

  water-rugs. The name suggests that these are rough-haired water-dogs.

  demi-wolves cross-bred from dog and wolf

94 *valued file* the catalogue re-arranged to show the prices

96 *house-keeper* domestic watchdog

99-100 *Particular addition from the bill | That writes them all alike.* The *valued file* gives back an individual title to each item, to discriminate it from the sameness of mere species, found in the *bill*.

101-2 *file . . . rank* (moving from the sense of *file* in line 94 above to the military sense)

106 *in his life* while he lives

111 *tugged with* knocked about by

112 *set* gamble

115 *distance* (1) dissension; (2) space between combatants in fencing

116-17 *every minute of his being thrusts | Against my near'st of life* his very existence is like a sword thrusting against my vitals (picking up second sense in *distance* above, line 115)

118 *With bare-faced power* using my power as King quite openly

119 *bid my will avouch it* justify it by my impulse

120 *For* for the sake of; on account of

123 *I to your assistance do make love* I woo your power to come to my aid

127 *Your spirits shine through you.* Say no more; I see your resolution in your eyes.

129 *the perfect spy o'the time* perhaps the Third Murderer (who appears in III.3); but may simply mean 'the perfect report (espial) on the time (to commit the murder)'

131 *something* somewhat; some distance
   thought be it understood

132 *I require a clearness* I must be able to clear myself of any suspicion

133 *rubs nor botches* unevennesses, clumsy work

137 *Resolve yourselves apart* go away and make up your minds

III.2 The development in Macbeth is shown in domestic as well as political relationship. He dominates his wife's conduct with eloquent restlessness. Note also the corresponding change in Lady Macbeth.

4 *Naught's had, all's spent* we have given everything, and achieved nothing

7 *by destruction dwell in doubtful joy* achieve, by destroying, only an apprehensive joy

9 *sorriest* most wretched

10 *Using* keeping company with

11 *them* (may imply a number of murders)

13 *scorched* slashed, as with a knife

14 *close* join up again (as a worm does)

15 *former tooth* her fangs, as dangerous as they were before the 'scorching'

16 *frame of things disjoint* the whole structure of the universe go to pieces
   both the worlds suffer terrestrial and celestial worlds perish

20 *to gain our peace, have sent to peace* (we killed to gain peace of mind, but have only managed to give peace to our victims)

21   *the torture of the mind* (the bed is a rack)

22   *In restless ecstasy* in a frenzy of delirium

23   *fitful* marked by paroxysms or fits

25   *foreign levy* an army levied abroad

27   *rugged* (monosyllabic here)

30   *Let your remembrance apply* remember to pay special attention (*remembrance* has four syllables)

31   *Present him eminence* give him special honour

32–3   *Unsafe the while that we | Must lave our honours in these flattering streams.* The time is so unsafe for us that we can only keep our honours clean by washing them in flattery. ('A grotesque and violent figure which shows the impatient self-contempt of the speaker' – Kittredge.)

34   *vizards* false faces

38   *nature's copy* (1) the form that Nature has given them by copying the first creation: 'particular casts from Nature's mould'; (2) copyhold – a lease that can be broken

40   *jocund.* Note how joy is associated with death.

41   *cloistered.* The bat flies in and around buildings rather than in the open air.

42   *shard-borne* (1) born (sic) in dung; (2) borne aloft by its wing-cases

44   *note* (1) memory; (2) sound

45   *dearest chuck* (a grim intimacy)

46–7   *Come, seeling night, | Scarf up the tender eye of pitiful day.* Night is to hide the dreadful deed from daylight as the falconer *seels* or sews up the eyes of the hawk.

47   *Scarf up* blindfold

48   *bloody and invisible.* The falconer's hand is *bloody* (from the *seeling*) and is *invisible* to the hawk, now effectively blinded.

49   *that great bond* the moral law; or perhaps the sixth commandment, against killing. (Perhaps *bond* should be pronounced *band*, to rhyme with *hand*.)

50   *pale* (1) paled, fenced-in – following a secondary sense in *bond* (=bondage); (2) tender-hearted, a creature seeing through the 'tender eye of pitiful day'

50   *thickens* grows dense, opaque, dim

53   *to their preys do rouse* bestir themselves to hunt their prey

III.3   The altercation between the Third Murderer and the other two is a nice illustration of the dependence of tyranny on mistrust.

3   *offices* duties

4   *To the direction just* exactly as required
      stand 'wait here'; or 'join our side'

6   *lated* belated; overtaken by the night

10   *within the note of expectation* in the list of expected guests

12-14   *but he does usually. | So all men do, from hence to the palace gate | Make it their walk.* F has a comma after 'usually', allowing one to phrase it: 'he does . . . (so all men . . .) make it their walk'.

16   *Let it come down* let 'the rain of blood' come down

III.4   This scene gives the success and failure of Macbeth's assault on 'royalty' its climactic expression, and makes the contrast between false order and true order quite explicit. It should recall the earlier banquet which welcomed Duncan to Inverness (I.7) - a true image of kingly *content*; and it also looks forward to the inhuman banquet of the Witches in IV.1. The final episode, with the King and Queen abandoned and guilt-oppressed amid the relics of their feasting, gives eloquent visual expression to the meaning of their fates.

1   *degrees* rank, position at table. The feast is a symbol of order.

1-2   *At first | And last* once and for all

2, 6, 8   *welcome.* 'The first three speeches of the King and Queen end with the word "welcome"' (Kittredge).

3   *mingle with society* leave the dais; move round among the guests

5   *state* canopied throne
           in best time when it is most appropriate

9–10   *See, they encounter thee with their hearts' thanks; | Both
           sides are even.* Perhaps some stage direction is necessary
           here to indicate the mode by which the guests show
           their *even* (equivalent) response to the Queen. On the
           other hand, the *even* is often taken to refer to the table:
           both sides are full, so *Here I'll sit i'the midst.*

18   *the nonpareil* without an equal

20   *fit* fever of anxiety
           perfect completely secure, healthy

21   *Whole* unbroken (in surface)
           founded secure

22   *As broad and general* as wide-embracing
           casing enveloping

23   *cabined, cribbed, confined, bound in* imprisoned (the
           'damnable iteration' conveys Macbeth's hysterical in-
           tensity)

24   *saucy* importunate

24, 25   *safe* (heavily ironic)

28   *worm* little serpent

31   *hear ourselves* hear one another. (Notice the assimilation
           of the King and the murderer.)

32   *give the cheer* welcome your guests

32–4   *The feast is sold | That is not often vouched, while 'tis
           a-making, | 'Tis given with welcome.* It is merely a com-
           mercial affair if the hosts do not punctuate the feast
           with assertions of welcome.

34–5   *To feed were best at home; | From thence, the sauce to
           meat is ceremony.* If feeding is the sole concern, home is
           the best place for it; away from home it is ceremony
           that makes a feast worthwhile. (*Ceremony*, pronounced
           'seer-money', seems to have been trisyllabic in Shake-
           speare's day.)

36   *remembrancer* an officer whose original function was to
           remind his superior of his duties

37   *good digestion wait on appetite* enjoy whatever you eat

39 *our country's honour* all the nobility of Scotland

40 *graced* (1) our guest of honour; (2) full of grace

41 *challenge for* reproach with

48 *done this* (1) killed Banquo; (2) filled up the seat

49 *Thou canst not say I did it.* He defends himself by saying that he did not strike the actual blow against Banquo.

54 *upon a thought* in a moment

59 *proper stuff* stuff and nonsense

61 *air-drawn* sketched out of air; pulled through air

62 *flaws* sudden gusts (of passion)

63–5 *Impostors to true fear, would well become | A woman's story at a winter's fire, | Authorized by her grandam.* These are not concerned with reality, but are simply passions such as would be appropriate to a dramatic rendering of a ghost-story – one whose credibility rests on the authority of an old woman.

65 *Authorized* (accent on second syllable)

70–72 *If charnel-houses and our graves must send | Those that we bury, back, our monuments | Shall be the maws of kites* if the dead return from normal burial-places, we will have to throw their bodies for birds of prey to eat

70 *charnel-houses* bone-stores

75 *Ere humane statute purged the gentle weal* before the benevolence of law cleansed society and made it gentle

80 *mortal murders* fatal wounds

81 *push us from our stools* (1) occupy the seat at the feast; (2) take over the succession to the throne

90 *we thirst* we are anxious to drink

91 *And all to all* let all men drink to everyone

  Our duties and the pledge! We drink our homage to you, and the toast you have just proposed.

94 *speculation* power of knowing what you see

100 *armed* armour-plated

  Hyrcan. Tigers in Latin literature were often said to come from Hyrcania, by the Caspian Sea.

101 *nerves* sinews

104 *If trembling I inhabit then* if I live in a trembling body, if I harbour trembling

105 *The baby of a girl* (a multiplication of unmanly types; *baby* is sometimes thought to refer to a doll)

108 *displaced* removed

109 *With most admired disorder* with this strange disordering of your wits

110 *overcome us like a summer's cloud* bring sudden gloom over us, as a cloud may do in a sunlit day

111–12 *strange | Even to the disposition that I owe* seem unlike the brave person I have supposed myself to be

118 *Stand not upon the order of your going* (an exit in strong contrast to the entrance, III.4.1). The *disorder* in Macbeth's mind has produced social disorder.

121 *It will have blood, they say; blood will have blood.* The F punctuation (followed here – most editors put the semi-colon before *they*) can be interpreted as an initial, half-reverie, statement of the proverb (from Genesis 9.6) followed by a more complete repetition and explanation of it.

122–5 *Stones have been known to move and trees to speak* . . . (the whole of nature conspires to reveal the unnatural sin of murder)

123 *Augurs* prophecies
understood relations either (1) reports properly comprehended; or (2) connexions elucidated

124 *maggot-pies, and choughs* magpies and crows

127 *How sayst thou, that* what do you say to the fact that

130–31 *There's not a one of them, but in his house | I keep a servant fee'd* (an explanation of how he heard 'by the way')

132 *betimes* either (1) early in the morning; or (2) while there is yet time

139 *Which must be acted ere they may be scanned.* There is not time to con the part, it must be put into performance at once.

140 *season* preservative

141–2   *My strange and self-abuse | Is the initiate fear that wants hard use* my strange self-deception (seeing Banquo's ghost) is only due to the terror of the beginner who lacks toughening experience

143   *young in deed* novices in crime

III.5   One of the scenes most regularly suspected of being interpolations. Hecat is a new and hitherto unannounced character, and the nature of the Witches seems to have been changed; Macbeth is now viewed as an *adept* or disciple of the Witches, not a victim. On the other hand, the end of Hecat's speech catches at a principal theme of the whole play (see Introduction, p. 21) and her speech, though distinguished from the Witch-utterances by its iambic (rather than trochaic) rhymes, is poetically very accomplished.

2   *beldams* hags

7   *close* secret

15   *Acheron* hell

21   *Unto a dismal and a fatal end* with a view to a disastrous and fatal conclusion

24   *profound* with deep or powerful qualities

32   *security* culpable absence of anxiety (it is a key word in the play; see Introduction, p. 21)

36   (stage direction) *Sing*. The full text of a song with this first line is found in the MS play *The Witch*, by Middleton, and in Davenant's version of *Macbeth*. The Davenant text of the song is far from clear, and I have been obliged to seek for light in the Middleton text. The essential matter seems to be that it is a *divided* song, with 'voices off' calling on Hecat to join them in their aerial exercises. Music in the air must be heard before Hecat says 'Hark! I am called.' Shakespeare's *Macbeth*, indeed, needs no more than the first two lines of the song, to be followed by Hecat's flying exit. The text of

the full song given here is conflated from the Middleton and Davenant versions:

> *Song in the air*
> Come away, come away;
> Hecat, Hecat, come away.

HECAT

> I come, I come, I come, I come,
> With all the speed I may,
> With all the speed I may.
> Where's Stadlin?

(IN THE AIR)

> Here.

HECAT

> Where's Puckle?

(IN THE AIR)

> Here.
> And Hoppo too, and Helwaine too.
> We lack but you, we lack but you.
> Come away, make up the count.

HECAT

> I will but 'noint, and then I mount.

(IN THE AIR)

> Here comes down one to fetch his dues,
> A kiss, a coll, a sip of blood;
> And why thou stay'st so long I muse,
> Since the air's so sweet and good.

> *A spirit like a cat descends*

HECAT

> O, art thou come?
> What news, what news?

SPIRIT

> All goes still to our delight:
> Either come, or else
> Refuse, refuse.

HECAT

> Now I am furnished for the flight.

(*going up*)
Now I go, now I fly,
Malkin my sweet spirit, and I.
O what a dainty pleasure 'tis
To ride in the air
When the moon shines fair,
And sing, and dance, and toy, and kiss,
Over woods, high rocks, and mountains,
Over seas, our mistress' fountains,
Over steeples, towers, and turrets,
We fly by night 'mong troops of spirits.
No ring of bells to our ears sounds,
No howls of wolves, no yelps of hounds,
No, not the noise of water's breach,
Or cannon's throat, our height can reach.
(IN THE AIR)
No ring of bells etc.

III.6   In terms of the intrigue, this scene exists to tell us that
Macbeth's purpose of sending to Macduff, mentioned
in III.4.129, has now been fulfilled; and that Macduff
has fled to England. But the speech of Lennox serves
further – as an exposé of the mind under tyranny, reduced to irony as its sole mode of opposition – to present the claustrophobic atmosphere of Scotland and the
scent of freedom (in the downright refusal of Macduff).

1-2   *My former speeches have but hit your thoughts,* | *Which
can interpret further.* What I have already said to you
has matched what you think; and you must draw your
own conclusions. (The whole conversation is an example of the reserve that must accompany tyranny.)

2   *Only I say* I only say

3, 5   *gracious Duncan . . . right valiant Banquo.* No doubt
these are Macbeth's phrases.

10   *fact* crime

12   *pious* (1) religious; (2) son-like

15–16   *For 'twould have angered any heart alive | To hear the men deny't.* He killed them so that men should not be angered by hearing them deny it.

21   *broad words* unrestrained talk

22   *tyrant's* (Lennox is now talking 'broad' himself)

27   *the most pious Edward* (Edward the Confessor)

28   *malevolence of fortune* his loss of his throne

30   *to pray the holy king, upon his aid* to beg Edward for assistance

34   *Give to our tables meat* hold open feasts

36   *Do faithful homage and receive free honours.* The implication is that under Macbeth the homage paid to the sovereign is hypocritical, the honours not *free*, but bought by servility.

37   *this report.* If the *King* in line 38 is Macbeth (see note on that line) then the report might be (a) that of Macduff's flight or (b) that of Malcolm's reception in England. The syntax would suggest (a); but this has the disadvantage of contradicting IV.1.141 (where Macbeth appears ignorant of Macduff's flight) and it seems preferable to understand (b) here. We may, if we wish, imagine that Shakespeare's original draft ran straight on from *respect* (line 29) to *And* (line 37).

38   *the.* The F reading *their* suggests that the king is Edward; and this would make perfect sense as far as the Lord's speech is concerned. But the *he* of Lennox's reply must be Macbeth; and if this is so, the *King* of line 38 must also be Macbeth.

40–41   *And with an absolute 'Sir, not I!' | The cloudy messenger turns me his back.* The messenger turns back towards his master, bearing Macduff's absolute 'Not I' answer.

41   *cloudy* lowering, scowling
       me (ethic dative; only present to give emphasis)

42   *hums* says 'hum' ('um', 'umph')

43   *clogs* impedes my advancement. (Messengers bearing bad news did not recommend themselves to tyrants.)

44   *him* Macduff
       distance (between himself and Macbeth)

IV.1   Usually set in a cavern, because of the 'pit of Acheron' reference in III.5; but line 46 seems to imply a building with a door. The scene bears the same (generative) relationship to the second half of the play as do the prophecies of I.3 to the first half. The iambic speeches, 39–43, 124–31, are often thought interpolated; they exist to justify the song and dance, and obviously differ in their tone – more delicate and pleasant – from the rest of the Witch material.

1	*brinded cat* streaked cat (the First Witch's familiar)
2	*hedge-pig* hedgehog
3	*Harpier* (the third familiar – a word formed from *Harpy*)
7	*thirty-one* (meaning, I suppose, 'one full month')
8	*Sweltered venom, sleeping got* venom sweated out during sleep
10, 20 etc.	*Double, double, toil and trouble* let toil and trouble be doubled in the world
12	*fenny* living in fen or marshland
15	*tongue of dog* (appears in this sinister catalogue because of Shakespeare's abhorrence of canine fawning)
16	*fork* forked tongue
	blind-worm slow-worm (now known to be venom-less)
17	*howlet* young owl
18	*For* in order to produce
19	*boil and bubble* (imperatives)
23	*Witch's mummy* mummified fragments of a witch
	maw and gulf gullet and stomach
24	*ravined* having finished devouring his prey
25	*digged i'the dark* (at the time when it was most noxious)
26	*Liver* (supposed to be the seat of the passions) *of blaspheming Jew* ('blaspheming' because he denies Christ's divinity)
27	*Gall* secretion of the liver; rancour
	slips seedlings
	yew (because poisonous)
28	*Slivered in the moon's eclipse* torn from the tree at a particularly baneful time

29   *Turk . . . Tartar's* (like *Jew*, line 26, and *babe*, line 30, attractive to witches because unchristened)

31   *Ditch-delivered by a drab* born in a ditch, the child of a harlot

32   *slab* viscous

33   *chaudron* entrails

34   *cauldron.* The Elizabethan pronunciation of *cauldron* (as of *vault*, *falcon*, *caulk* etc.) kept the 'l' silent, so that the rhyme with *chaudron* was perfect.

37   *baboon's blood.* Hot and lustful; and therefore only cooling to the unnaturally fiery. *Baboon* has accent on first syllable.

38   (stage direction) *Enter Hecat and the other three Witches.* The song 'Black Spirits' (as it appears in Middleton's *The Witch*) does not require more than three performers; though the refrain might be thought to deserve a larger body. If a chorus of six Witches seems offensive we can read (as is sometimes done): 'Enter Hecat [to] the other three Witches', and so avoid increasing the Witch population.

43   (stage direction) *song.* The full text of a song with this first line is found in the MS play *The Witch*, by Middleton, and in Davenant's printed version of *Macbeth*; I quote the latter version, in which particular references to the plot of *The Witch* have been deleted:

HECATE

    Black spirits, and white,
    Red spirits, and grey,
    Mingle, mingle, mingle,
    You that mingle may.

FIRST WITCH

    Tiffin, Tiffin, keep it stiff in;
    Firedrake, Puckey, make it lucky;
    Liar Robin, you must bob in.

CHORUS

    Around, around, about, about;
    All ill come running in, all good keep out.

FIRST WITCH
  Here's the blood of a bat.
HECATE
  O, put in that, put in that.
SECOND WITCH
  Here's lizard's brain.
HECATE
  Put in a grain.
FIRST WITCH
  Here's juice of toad, here's oil of adder;
  That will make the charm grow madder.
SECOND WITCH
  Put in all these, 'twill raise the stench.
HECATE
  Nay, here's three ounces of a red-haired wench.
CHORUS
  Around, around, about, about;
  All ill come running in, all good keep out.

47   *secret, black, and midnight hags* wicked practitioners of
      'black' magic
51-9 *Though you untie the winds and let them fight* | ... *Even
      till destruction sicken* though order, civilization and the
      cosmos itself be destroyed
51   *Though you untie the winds.* Compare Revelation 7.1:
      'I saw four Angels stand on the four corners of the
      earth, holding the four winds of the earth.'
52   *yesty* foaming
54   *Though bladed corn be lodged* though new corn be beaten
      flat
57-8 *the treasure* | *Of nature's germens tumble all together*
      the patterns of creation fall into confusion
58   *nature's germens* the seeds or material essences of things
59   *Even till destruction sicken* (through over-eating)
62   *masters* the powers of Fate
67   *Thyself and office* thyself performing thy function
      (stage direction) *an Armed Head* (presumably that of

Macbeth himself, cut off by Macduff. The same property head would suffice for both occasions.)

73   *harped* guessed

75   (stage direction) *a Bloody Child* (presumably Macduff,
        'from his mother's womb untimely ripped')

83   *take a bond of fate* (a *bond* to 'make assurance double
        sure' – by disposing of Macduff (and the First Appari-
        tion's warning) *and* relying on 'none of woman born')

85   *thunder* (traditionally the expression of God's anger)
        (stage direction) *a Child crowned, with a tree in his hand*
        (Malcolm, advancing with a branch of Birnan Wood)

92   *Birnan.* F has 'Byrnam' here; the correct form in
        modern geography is *Birnam.* But Elizabethan authori-
        ties spell the word with an *n* ('Bernane' in Holinshed;
        'Brynnane' in Wintoun's *Original Chronicle*); and this
        is the form the Folio uses on every other occasion when
        the name appears (IV.1.97; V.3.2 and 60; V.4.3;
        V.5.34 and 44; V.6.69). We must assume that the *m* is
        an error here, and that *Birnan* is the correct Shake-
        spearian form.

93-101 *That will never be ... | Can tell so much.* As Kittredge
        notes, Macbeth's continuation of the rhymed speech-
        form of the Apparition implies his absorption into that
        world of false 'security'. Note also his third-person
        reference to himself in line 97.

94   *impress* conscript

95   *bodements* auguries

96   *Rebellious dead.* Theobald's emendation 'Rebellion's
        head' has been generally accepted. It takes up, very
        neatly, the idea of 'where conspirers are' above. But the
        idea of *dead* is much closer to 'Unfix ... root', which
        can be seen to resurrect, in Macbeth's mind, the obses-
        sion with Banquo that runs through the scene. Banquo's
        ghost is a type of the rebellious – 'But now they rise ...
        and push us from our stools.'

99   *mortal custom* the custom of dying

110   (stage direction) *eight kings, and Banquo.* Banquo was

supposed to be the ancestor of the Stuart line. The eight kings would be Robert II, Robert III, James I, James II, James III, James IV, James V, Mary Queen of Scots. If we exclude Mary we have to include Walter Stewart (preceding Robert II).

116 *What, will the line stretch out to the crack of doom?* The Stuarts were proud of their unbroken lineal descent.

118 *a glass.* See Introduction, p. 30.

120 *That two-fold balls and treble sceptres carry* unite the crowns of England and Scotland (two-fold) and rule over Scotland, England, and Ireland (treble) – as did James I

122 *blood-boltered* his hair matted with blood

123 *for his* (claiming them as his descendants)

131 (stage direction) *The Witches dance.* This has been thought to be a further borrowing of music from *The Witch*, where we read 'here they dance the Witches' dance, and Exit'.

144-5 *The flighty purpose never is o'ertook | Unless the deed go with it.* We never realize our quickly vanishing purposes, unless we act at the very moment when we form these purposes.

148 *it* (what follows)

152 *trace* follow his tracks

154 *these gentlemen* (the 'two or three' of line 140)

IV.2 The scene breaks the grim descent of Macbeth by an interlude of domestic pathos. Both Ross and the nameless Messenger represent the natural sympathy of the oppressed under devilish pressure; their flight catches the weakness of any amiable ordinary individual under these circumstances and mirrors that of Macduff himself. Notice the descent from the 'honourable' murderers of Banquo to the brutish ruffians of this scene.

3-4 *when our actions do not, | Our fears do make us traitors.*

Macduff had *done* nothing traitorous; but his fear made him fly, and that is treachery.

10   *diminutive*. F uses the alternative form 'diminitive', the sound of which may be thought more appropriate to the meaning of the line.

11   *Her young ones in her nest* when her young ones are in the nest

14   *cuz* cousin, relative

15   *school yourself* teach yourself wisdom

17   *The fits o' the season* the unexpected convulsions of this time; ? what is fitting

18–19 *when we are traitors | And do not know, ourselves* when we are proclaimed as traitors and ourselves do not know that we are

19–20 *when we hold rumour | From what we fear* when all we have to hold on to are rumours, based on what we fear might be

22   *Each way and move*. The sense must be that the ignorantly fearful are at the mercy of the sea of fear; and are moved whatever way the sea moves. The language is not easy to fit into this; nor is the favourite emendation, 'Each way and none'.

29   *It would be my disgrace and your discomfort*. I should weep and so disgrace my manhood and distress you.

31   *Sirrah* (playful and affectionate address here)

36   *lime* birdlime (a sticky substance spread on branches, etc., to catch birds)
     gin snare

37   *Poor birds they are not set for* traps etc. are not set for a *poor* bird (as you call me – line 35)

42   *Then you'll buy 'em to sell again* you can't want all that number for your own consumption

43–4 *Thou speak'st with all thy wit; | And yet, i'faith, with wit enough for thee* you're not being very sensible; but sensible enough, I suppose, considering your age

48   *swears and lies* takes an oath and breaks it. (Lady Macduff is thinking of the marriage-oath to cherish the wife, as well as the oath to the King.)

59   *monkey* ('used tenderly, in the fantasticality of affection' - Kittredge)

66   *Though in your state of honour I am perfect* though I am perfectly acquainted with your honourable condition

71-2   *To do worse to you were fell cruelty, | Which is too nigh your person* it would be cruel to do more than frighten (i.e. harm) you, but such cruelty is close at hand

78   *womanly* womanish, feeble

80   *Where is your husband?* Coming from Macbeth, they must know that he is fled; but the Gestapo-type question may serve to incriminate Lady Macduff.

82, 83   *thou* (pejorative use of second person singular)

84   *fry* fish-spawn

IV.3   This, the longest scene in the play, performs a number of important structural functions. Of the three sections: (a) Malcolm's testing of Macduff, (b) the description of Edward the Confessor, and (c) the announcement of the slaughter of Macduff's family, the first is the most elaborate. It adds a further strand to the image of wariness and suspiciousness that characterizes tyranny. Malcolm's self-accusations describe the contrast between virtue and vice in kingship and Macduff's reactions are those of the ideal subject. Pious Edward touching for 'the Evil' is directly antithetical to Macbeth, and the doctor here should be contrasted with that in V.1. Macduff's reaction to Ross's bitter news exhibits full human range of feeling, of understanding and resolve to act. With piety to crown the effort, and with resolve to carry it forward, the counter-move against Macbeth is fully launched.

3   *mortal* deadly

4   *Bestride our down-fallen birthdom* stand over and defend the fallen body of the kingdom of our birth

6   *Strike heaven on the face* are as a slap in the face of goodness

6-8   *that it resounds | As if it felt with Scotland, and yelled out | Like syllable of dolour.* The noise of the blow against heaven echoes as if heaven were wailing for sorrow, like Scotland.

10 *to friend* favourable

14 *I am young; but ...* (1) although I am unimportant; (2) although I may seem innocent, I can understand that ...

15 *wisdom* it is wisdom

19–20 *recoil | In an imperial charge* be pushed backwards (morally) by the force of a royal command (image from gunnery)

21 *transpose* change (suspicion cannot make Macduff evil)

22 *the brightest* Lucifer

24 *so* (like grace)

25 *Perchance even there where I did find my doubts.* Macduff left his family in Macbeth's power. Was the betrayal of Malcolm to be the price of their safety? It was this thought that alerted Malcolm's *doubts*; and so Macduff will have to give up the *hope* of recovering his family.

26 *rawness* unprotected condition

27 *motives* (1) incentives to action; (2) objects *moving* one's emotions

29 *jealousies* suspicions

32–3 *tyranny ... thou ... thou* (Macbeth)

34 *affeered* legally confirmed

37 *to boot* as well

43 *gracious England* (Edward the Confessor, full of God's grace)

52 *opened* (as a bud opens – after *grafted*)

56, 57 *devil ... evils* (both monosyllables)

57 *top* surpass

58 *Luxurious* lustful

59 *Sudden* violent

64 *continent* (1) chaste; (2) restraining

65 *will* lust

67 *nature* human nature

71 *Convey* manage secretly

72   *hoodwink* blindfold

75   *greatness* (the great man, King Malcolm)

76   *so* (lustfully)

77   *ill-composed affection* disposition composed of evil elements

78   *staunchless* unquenchable

80   *his* (one man's)

81–2   *And my more-having would be as a sauce | To make me hunger more* the more I swallowed up, the sharper my appetite should be

82   *that* so that

86   *summer-seeming* that beseems or befits the summer of life (early manhood)

88   *foisons* abundance
      will passion

89   *Of your mere own* out of your own royal possessions
      portable bearable

93   *perseverance* (accented on the second syllable)

95–6   *abound | In the division of each several crime* I am fertile in the variations that can be produced in each separate (*several*) crime

98   *milk* (symbolizing, as already in the play, the innocence of natural relationships)

99   *Uproar* reduce to confusion

104   *untitled* with no legal right

107   *accused.* F *accust* may also be modernized as 'accursed'.

108   *does blaspheme his breed* is a slander to his family

111   *Died every day she lived* mortified herself daily (by religious exercises)

113   *breast* heart

115   *Child of integrity* produced by the integrity of your spirit

116   *black scruples* wicked suspicions

118   *trains* lures

126   *Unknown to woman* a virgin

131   *upon* against

135   *at a point* fully prepared

136–7   *and the chance of goodness | Be like our warranted quarrel!* May the chance of good success be proportionate to the justness of our cause

142–3   *convinces | The great assay of art* defeats the greatest efforts of medical skill

143–5   *but at his touch, | Such sanctity hath heaven given his hand, | They presently amend.* This is 'touching' for scrofula or 'the King's Evil', which began with Edward the Confessor and remained a prerogative of the English crown.

145   *presently* immediately

152   *mere* complete

153   *stamp* coin

160   *My countryman; but yet I know him not.* Malcolm presumably recognizes the 'Scottish' costume Ross is wearing.

162   *betimes* speedily

166–7   *nothing | But who knows nothing* no one except a person totally ignorant

169   *not marked* not noticed, because they are everywhere

170   *A modern ecstasy* a commonplace passion

173   *or ere they sicken* before they have time to fall ill

174   *Too nice* over-delicately phrased

175   *doth hiss the speaker* causes him to be hissed (because the news is out of date)

176   *teems* brings forth plenteously

177   *well . . . well* (because 'we use | To say the dead are well' (*Antony and Cleopatra*, II.5.33–4))

181–2   *the tidings | Which I have heavily borne.* Is this the heavy (sad) news of Macduff's family?

183   *out* in arms

188   *doff* take off

189   *Gracious England* (Edward the Confessor)

191   *none* there are none

192   *gives out* proclaims

195   *latch* catch

196–7   *a fee-grief | Due to some single breast* a grief with a single owner

206   *quarry* heap of dead animals

208   *pull your hat* (a conventional sign of grief)

215   *deadly* which would otherwise be fatal

217   *hell-kite* (that swooped on his chickens like a bird from hell)

219   *Dispute* struggle against

224   *for thee* because of thee. (Heaven would have intervened if Macduff's wickedness had not dissuaded it.) *Naught* wicked

231   *intermission* interval of time

236   *Our lack is nothing but our leave* we lack nothing but leave-taking

237   *ripe for shaking.* Perhaps a reminiscence from Nahum's prophecy of the fall of Nineveh: 'All thy strong aids are as fig trees with the first ripe figs: if they be stirred they fall into the mouth of the eater' (Nahum 3.12).

238   *Put on their instruments* (1) put on their weapons; (2) thrust us forward, as their agents

V.1   The scene re-enacts the life of bloodshed in terms of dream and hallucination (like a Noh play). It is the climax of Shakespeare's exploration of individual psychological secrets. The broken prose fragments of Lady Macbeth's speech measure the collapse of the human mind under inhuman pressures, while the Gentlewoman and the Doctor represent a choric norm. The Doctor (probably played by the same actor as the Doctor in IV.3) serves to focus the contrast between the English throne with its heaven-given medical powers, and the Scottish with its disease 'beyond my practice'.

5   *nightgown.* The Elizabethans slept without garments; the *nightgown* was equivalent to today's 'dressing-gown'. Re-enacts II.2.70.

8   *while* time

9–10   *A great perturbation in nature, to receive at once the benefit of sleep and do the effects of watching.* Lady Macbeth 'equivocates' with sleep.

10   *watching* waking

17-18 *having no witness to confirm my speech.* The Waiting-Gentlewoman is as suspicious as other subjects of tyranny.

31   *Yet* ('after all this washing' – Kittredge)

34   *One : two.* She recalls the timing of Duncan's murder.

35   *do't* murder Duncan

     Hell is murky ('a sudden glimpse into the abyss at her feet' – Dover Wilson)

42   *will these hands ne'er be clean?* This recalls (as so much of this scene does): 'A little water clears us of this deed; | How easy is it then!' (II.2.67–8).

50   *charged* burdened

63-4 *What's done cannot be undone* (a tragically ironic echo of III.2.12: 'what's done is done')

66   *Directly* immediately

67-8 *unnatural deeds | Do breed unnatural troubles.* Rebellion is 'unnatural', but is naturally produced when sovereigns commit unnatural deeds.

72   *Remove from her the means of all annoyance.* She is in a state of Despair (religiously conceived), and therefore must be considered a potential suicide.

74   *mated* confounded

V.2. 4   *alarm* the call to battle

10   *unrough* beardless

11   *Protest their first of manhood* proclaim that they are now (for the first time) acting as men

15   *distempered* diseased; perhaps 'swollen with dropsy'

17   *sticking* (like dried blood)

18   *minutely* occurring every minute (accented on first syllable)

19   *in* because of

22-3 *blame | His pestered senses to recoil and start* blame his afflicted nerves for jumping back and quivering

24-5   *When all that is within him does condemn | Itself for being there* when his whole nature revolts against his existence

27   *medicine* (1) drug; or more probably (2) physician (i.e. Malcolm)
     sickly weal the diseased commonwealth

28-9   *And with him pour we in our country's purge | Each drop of us* as men *purge* their disorders by bloodletting, so let us pour out our blood (in battle) to purge *the sickly weal*

30   *sovereign* (1) royal; (2) powerfully medicinal

V.3   The desperate 'security' of Macbeth, without hope, without companionship and therefore without meaning in his life – this is represented externally by the siege and internally by his despair. The Doctor serves, once again, to link the state of the mind with the state of the land, psychology with politics.

1   *them* (the thanes)

8   *English epicures.* From the traditional Scottish point of view the English are characterized by luxurious softness.

9   *sway* rule myself

11   *damn thee black.* Damned souls were thought to be black in colour.

12   *goose look* look of cowardly folly

14   *prick thy face and over-red thy fear* stick pins in your face and let the blood hide your pallor

15   *lily-livered* lacking in red-blooded bravery
     patch fool

16   *linen* bleached

20   *push* crisis

21   *chair.* Printed in F as *cheer*; the two words were pronounced alike; but *chair* seems the more apposite word to keep in line with *push* and *dis-seat*.

23   *sere, the yellow leaf* (a withered condition)

27-8   *breath | Which the poor heart would fain deny* words of allegiance which the emotions cannot accept as true – as in 'equivocation'. Compare Isaiah 29.13: 'This people when they be in trouble do honour me with their mouth and with their lips, but their heart is far from me.'

35   *more.* F prints the alternative Elizabethan form 'moe'.
        skirr scour

37   *your patient.* The *your* is emphatic, to make the contrast between Macbeth's treatment of the realm and the doctor's of Lady Macbeth – a contrast that recurs at lines 47–8 and 50–54.

38   *thick-coming* frequently appearing

42   *written* engraved

44   *stuffed* clogged (Kittredge notes the clogged movement of the line)

48   *staff* baton of office

50–51   *cast | The water* examine the urine

55   *senna.* F reads *cyme*; and this has been found in English, as an Anglicization of Greek/Latin *cyma*: the tender shoots of plants. But I suspect that the appearance of this rare word in the F text is an accident; and that Shakespeare's word was *cynne* – a variant spelling of *senna* – which has the right meaning and the right value for scansion.

56   *scour* (1) remove rapidly (as *skirr* above); (2) cleanse the body by purgatives; (3) also used of cleaning armour

58   *it* (the piece of armour)

62   *Profit* (the traditional motive of doctors)

V.4   Now all the nobles we have known from earlier in the play have joined Malcolm's army. Notice the humility of their grasp on the future, to be compared with Macbeth's furious indifference.

2   *chambers* (perhaps bedchambers – they were not safe for Duncan)

5   *shadow* conceal

6   *discovery* spying

10   *setting down before't* besieging it

11   *there is advantage to be given* opportunity (to escape) is afforded them

12   *more and less* great men and humble men

14-15 *Let our just censures | Attend the true event* if our judgements are to be accurate they must wait to know the true end of the affair

18   *What we shall say we have, and what we owe* (the difference between talk and true possession – *owe*=own)

20   *But certain issue strokes must arbitrate* only blows decide the real future

V.5   The alternation of scenes in Act V makes this a natural extension of V.3. The supreme horror of the heart numbed by despair appears in the reaction to Lady Macbeth's death. From this time forth Macbeth's life is a waiting for the end.

5   *farced* stuffed. The F word 'forc'd' is sometimes defended as having the sense of 'reinforced'; but this meaning is only doubtfully attested. In view of the food images in the line before it seems best to take 'forc'd' as the common Elizabethan variant of *farced*.

6   *dareful* in open battle

10   *cooled* chilled with terror

11   *my fell of hair* the hair on my skin

12   *dismal treatise* a story of disaster

13   *supped full with* had my fill of. The metaphor takes us back to III.4.

14   *familiar*. Is there a reminiscence here of the Witches' *familiars*?

17   *should*. I think this means 'certainly would' rather than 'ought to have'.

     hereafter at some time – what does the actual moment matter?

18   *There would have been a time for such a word.* His mind moves back from the meaninglessness of any future to the meaningfulness of the past. 'At one time I could have responded to such a word (announcement).' The transition to the following line implies the transition from that past to this present.

20   *in this petty pace* in the petty manner of this pace. I assume that he paces as he speaks.

21   *To the last syllable of recorded time* till time reaches the last recorded word

23   *dusty death* death, which is a matter of 'dust to dust'

24   *shadow.* Suggested by *lighted . . . candle* and suggesting *player* in its turn. Compare Job 8.9: 'We are but of yesterday . . . our days upon earth are but a shadow.' *a poor player.* The actor is *poor* (i.e. worthy of pity) because his voice soon ceases to be heard.

25   *frets* expresses discontent and disdain

40   *cling* shrink up, wither *sooth* true

42   *pull in* rein in. (Many editors have preferred to emend to 'pall in'.)

V.6   Usually printed as four separate scenes, but logic would demand either more divisions (e.g. at lines 23 and 73) or none at all. The battle is a series of spotlights but the action must be continuous. The alternation between sides that has marked Act V so far now speeds up, till the two blur into one victory and one defeat.

2   *uncle* (Seyward)

4   *battle* battalion *we.* Malcolm now assumes the royal *we.*

10   *harbingers* forerunners

11   *They have tied me to a stake* (like a bear being baited)

12   *the course* (one round of dogs versus bear)

30   *undeeded* without any deeds performed

34   *gently rendered* surrendered without fighting

39   *strike beside us* miss intentionally

40   *the Roman fool* (some Stoic suicide – e.g. Brutus)

48   *intrenchant* that cannot be gashed

53   *angel* demon
       still always

58   *juggling* deceiving, cheating

59   *palter with us in a double sense* equivocate by double
       meanings

64   *monsters* prodigies, marvels

65   *Painted upon a pole* on a painted cloth set up on a pole
       (in front of the booth)

71   *try the last* make the final test (of fate)

73   (stage direction) *Exeunt fighting. Alarums. Enter fighting,
       and Macbeth slain.* It is not clear why F has these two
       contradictory directions. Perhaps they *Exeunt* from the
       main stage and then *Enter* on the inner stage (or balcony)
       where a curtain can be drawn to conceal Macbeth's
       body.
       (stage direction) *Retreat* the trumpet-call for the end of
       the fighting

75   *go off* die (perhaps a stage metaphor=exit)

87   *hairs* (with pun on *heirs*)

91   *parted* departed
       score reckoning, account

93   *stands* (presumably the head is on a pole)

95   *pearl* (suggested probably by the idea of 'peers' and by
       the pearls which surround a crown)

100   *reckon with your several loves* add up what we owe to
       each individual

102   *Scotland* (? the King of Scotland)

104   *Which would be planted newly with the time* which
       ought to be given a new beginning in a new age

107   *ministers* agents

109   *by self and violent hands* by her own violent hands

111   *by the grace of Grace* with God's help

112   *measure, time, and place* with due order in every
       dimension

AN ACCOUNT OF THE TEXT

The Names of the Characters

The Folio's names for the characters in *Mabeth* are consist-
ent and do not require emendation to make them intelligible;
but editors have regularly changed some of them in the
interest of historical accuracy or modern usage. In the Folio
Lady Macbeth is regularly referred to as *Lady*, Duncan as
King, Lady Macduff as *Wife* (*Macduff's Wife* in the Entry
to IV.2), and these I have preserved as possible indicators of
the author's sense of their roles. To modernize names is to
give historical specificity to persons and places that have
their meaning inside the play and not in atlases and text-
books. 'Banwho' is no doubt the correct phonetic rendering
of Banquo (= Banquho) but it would be mere pedantry to
print it. Shakespeare's *Hecat* (two syllables) is not the
classical Hecate (three syllables); his *Birnan* is not the
Birnam that can be found on a map. His *Cathness* and
Menteth are not the modern Caithness and Menteith, but
names he found in Holinshed and fitted (in these forms)
into his versification

The 'Other Murderers' who appear in the list are those
who murder Lady Macduff and her son. These are dramati-
cally distinct from the 'Three Murderers' with whom Macbeth arranges the murder of Banquo. The 'Three Other
Witches' who enter with Hecat at IV.1.38 seem to be
different from the Weird Sisters found elsewhere.

The Source of the Text

Macbeth first appeared in the collected volume of Shakespeare's plays (1623), the so-called First Folio. The text
found there has been the subject of much suspicion (like

almost everything in that famous volume). The play is shorter than any other tragedy (about 2,100 lines). This does not mean, however, that it has been shortened. The text as we have it is entirely intelligible, orderly and coherent (Acts and scenes are regularly marked). This means that there has not been much room for displays of textual ingenuity. W. W. Greg, *The Shakespeare First Folio* (1955), summarizes the standard assumptions. It is usually supposed that the printers of the Folio set their text from the theatre's prompt-book (or a transcript of it). The editor's function is therefore to follow the Folio text except where there are manifest printing errors (not collated below) or where the intention of the passage seems to be contradicted by the Folio reading. A list of these latter cases is given. The alternative reading printed is that of the Folio, except that long 's' [ʃ] is not used.

THE INTEGRITY OF THE TEXT

The songs and associated dialogue in III.5 and IV.1 (called 'interpolations' above (headnote to III.5)) have recently been redescribed as 'contributions' by Thomas Middleton, acting as Shakespeare's collaborator (this has led to even larger claims for Middleton's authorship in *Macbeth*.) The Oxford editors and Nicholas Brooke have responded to this claim by putting into the text all the elaborations of the Folio that appear in the manuscript of Middleton's *The Witch* and in Davenant's version of *Macbeth*, with flying ascents and descents, choral interludes and a singing cat (whose Muse is 'mews').

It is clear that these operatic confections are part of the stage history of *Macbeth* (which continued to rely on the charms of 'new songs' to sell new editions up to 1785), and it is equally clear that Shakespeare's text cannot be treated as purely literary, quite uncontaminated by stage history. But we do not know at what point they joined that history (the relationship of song texts to play texts is everywhere obscure and little understood). Clearly, the taste represented by these 'interpolations' or 'contributions' is unique in the Folio, and no argument has so far been produced to explain why these Purcellian or baroque accents appear in contradiction of the 'Shakespearean' music audible elsewhere in *Macbeth*. It still seems best, therefore, not to rewrite the Folio text in order to accommodate them.

COLLATIONS

I.1. 8–9   1. I come, *Gray-Malkin.*
          All. Padock calls anon: faire is foule, and foule is
          faire

I.2.   0   (stage direction) *King Duncan, Malcolm*] *King
          Malcome*

      14   quarrel] Quarry

      45   (stage direction) *Exit Captain with Attendants*] not
          in F

      58   point-rebellious,] Point, rebellious (most editors:
          point rebellious,)

I.3.96–7   as hail | Came] as Tale | Can (Johnson: as tale | Came)

     126   (stage direction) *They walk apart*] not in F

I.4.   0   (stage direction) *King Duncan, Lennox*] *King, Lenox*

       2   Are] Or

I.5. 15   human-kindness] humane kindnesse

I.6.   0   (stage direction) *King Duncan, Malcolm*] *King,
          Malcolme*

       9   most] must

      10   (stage direction) *Enter Lady Macbeth*] *Enter Lady*

      31   (stage direction) *He kisses her*] not in F

I.7.   6   shoal] Schoole

      28   (stage direction) *Enter Lady Macbeth*] *Enter Lady*

      66   a-fume] a Fume (other editors follow this F
          reading)

II.1. 30   (stage direction) *Exit Banquo and Fleance*] *Exit
          Banquo*

      55   strides] sides

      56   sure] sowre

      57   way they] they may

II.2. 0   (stage direction) *Enter Lady Macbeth*] *Enter Lady*

       8   (stage direction) MACBETH (*within*)] *Enter Macbeth*

      13   (stage direction) *Enter Macbeth, carrying two
          bloodstained daggers*] not in F

      63   green one red] Greene one, Red
          (stage direction) *Enter Lady Macbeth*] *Enter Lady*

II.3. 19 (stage direction) *He opens the gate*] not in F
       39 (stage direction) *Enter Macbeth*] F places after line 38
       70 (stage direction) *Exeunt Macbeth and Lennox*] F places after *awake* (line 70)
       77 (stage direction) *Enter Lady Macbeth*] *Enter Lady*
      122 (stage direction) *Lady Macbeth is taken out*] not in F
      131 (stage direction) *Exeunt all but Malcolm and Donalbain*] *Exeunt*

III.1. 11 (stage direction) *Lady Macbeth, Lennox*] *Lady Lenox*
        44 (stage direction) *Exeunt Lords and Lady Macbeth*] *Exeunt Lords*
        69 seeds] as in F (most editors: seed)
       139 (stage direction) *Exeunt Murderers*] not in F
       141 (stage direction) *Exit*] *Exeunt*

III.3. 16 (stage direction) *They attack Banquo*] not in F
        18 (stage direction) *Banquo falls. Fleance escapes*] not in F

III.4.   0 (stage direction) *Lady Macbeth, Ross*] *Lady, Rosse*
         4 (stage direction) *He walks around the tables*] not in F
        12 (stage direction) *He rises and goes to the Murderer*] not in F
        38 (stage direction) *Enter the Ghost of Banquo and sits in Macbeth's place*] F places after 'it' (line 36)
        72 (stage direction) *Exit Ghost*] not in F
       106 (stage direction) *Exit Ghost*] not in F
       143 in deed] indeed

III.6. 24 son] Sonnes
        38 the] their

IV.1.   43 (stage direction) *Exeunt Hecat and the other three Witches*] not in F
        58 germens] Germaine
        92 Birnan] Byrnam
        96 Rebellious dead] as in F (most editors: Rebellion's head)
       105 (stage direction) *Hautboys*] F places after 'this' (line 105)

IV.1. 110   (stage direction) *and Banquo; the last king*] *and Banquo last,*

IV.2. 79   (stage direction) *Enter Murderers*] F places after 'faces' (line 79)

    83   shag-haired] shagge-ear'd

    84   (stage direction) *He stabs him*] not in F

    85   (stage direction) *Son dies. Exit Wife crying 'Murder'*] *Exit crying Murther*

IV.3. 4   down-fallen] downfall

    15   deserve] discerne

   133   thy] they

   145   (stage direction) *Exit Doctor*] F places after 'amend' (line 145)

   234   tune] time

V.1. 18   (stage direction) *Enter Lady Macbeth*] *Enter Lady*

V.3. 19   (stage direction) *Exit Servant*] not in F

    21   chair . . . dis-seat] cheere . . . dis-eate

    39   Cure her] Cure

    55   senna] Cyme

    60   (stage direction) *Exit*] not in F

    62   (stage direction) *Exit*] *Exeunt*

V.5. 5   farced] *forc'd*

    7   (stage direction) *A cry within of women*] F places after *noise* (line 7)

    8   (stage direction) *Exit*] not in F

    15   (stage direction) *Enter Seyton*] not in F

V.6. 10   F marks a new scene at this point

    73   (stage direction) *Exit Macduff*] not in F

'Mislineation' in Macbeth

'Mislineation' is the name given to a printing of verse-lines in a form which seems to the most experienced readers to run counter to the author's usual procedure, requiring the modern editor to relineate the verse (there is an elaborate discussion of the topic in Brooke's edition, Appendix A). A fairly obvious example occurs in *Macbeth* I.4.23–8, which appears in the Folio as follows:

Macb. The seruice, and the loyaltie I owe,/
In doing it, payes it selfe.
Your Highnesse part,/is to receiue our Duties:
And our Duties/are to your Throne, and State,
Children, and Seruants;/which doe but what they should,
By doing euery thing/safe toward your Loue
And Honor.
King. Welcome hither:/

Editors normally reline this, the new line-ends coming at the points where I have inserted the oblique strokes. The reasons which lie behind their efforts are both aesthetic and arithmetical. The lines as printed run oddly and clumsily; the sense rhythms contradict the verse-rhythms quite arbitrarily. Moreover, it can be noticed that the completion of the half-line, with subsequent division into full lines, produces a neat metrical ending (a single and complete line of verse). The sum adds up. But no more than arithmetical regularity would have been achieved, if the sense-rhythms had not also been made to run more easily; since they do so here, this may be taken as a confirmation of the propriety of the relineation.

The difficulty of recognizing mislineation in Shakespeare is usually greater than this. There is no necessity for his lines to run with complete regularity; and certainly there is no rule that interjections or new speeches should run to the end of the line (on this matter, see Fredson Bowers, 'Establishing Shakespeare's Text: Notes on Short Lines and the Problems of Verse Division', *Studies in Bibliography*, 33 (1980), 74–130). Shakespeare wrote his plays to be spoken rather than written and no doubt thought of his rhythmic units in terms of the voice rather than the page. The editor is not dealing with material which aspires towards any single and definite printed form. This is particularly obvious when the editor has to deal with problems of verse or prose. It hardly helps here to know that Shakespeare did not think in terms of 'Now I'll write in prose', 'I think I'll write a few lines in verse here', but moved effortlessly all the way along a scale from the most rhythmical to the least rhythmical units. Conversations like that between young Macduff and his mother (Act IV, scene 2), mainly in short units, raise really insoluble editorial problems when lines of the conversation fall into fairly obvious blank-verse units: 'Thou speak'st with all thy wit', says Macduff's wife, 'And yet, i'faith, with wit enough for thee.' Is this verse or prose? The proper answer is 'Neither; it is speech'. The Folio prints this example as verse, perhaps for no very good reason; and I have been content to follow it; but most editors have changed it to prose.

Macbeth is a play with a great deal of mislineation; and it is often suggested that this proves that it was rewritten or otherwise cut about. A number of reasons for this emerge, however, which have nothing to do with revision or rewriting. The Folio is printed in double columns, on a narrower allowance of space for long lines than in modern reprints. This leads to a number of what may be called 'normal' mislineations. The end of Act II, scene 2, is printed in two passages of half-lines instead of whole lines (lines 65–9 and 73, 74) partly to leave space for the *Knock* and *Exeunt* stage-directions on the right-hand side of the column. I.3.77 is similarly divided into two, to allow space for the stage-direction *Witches vanish*.

These are considerations which apply to all the plays; but there are further considerations which narrow the field of inquiry. The plays which W. W. Greg's *The Shakespeare First Folio* mentions as posing particular problems of lineation are *Antony and Cleopatra*, *Timon of Athens*, and *Coriolanus*. Add *Macbeth* to these and we have a probably complete list of the plays that Shakespeare wrote between 1606 and 1608. The verse of these plays has in common a new looseness of structure or fluidity of movement, and this may have imposed on either Shakespeare *or* the transcriber *or* the compositors (or all three) problems of conveying the 'feel' of the verse on to the page. Certainly there is evidence that the Folio compositors found it difficult to handle their material. The rhetoric of reported action, as it appears in *Macbeth*, has an individual rhythmic character, including a formal use of quasi-Virgilian short lines ('Till he faced the slave'; 'I cannot tell'; 'And fan our people cold'; 'Craves composition'; 'My liege') which seems to have confused the compositor of Act I, scene 2, and Act I, scene 4, as it confuses modern editors. Again the fragmentary whispered conversation of Act II, scene 2, in the style of

LADY

  Did not you speak?

MACBETH   When?

LADY   Now.

MACBETH   As I descended?

imposed its own problems, and produced its own crop of irregularities. It is worth noticing that the Witch-scenes, with their clearly marked short lines, yield hardly any examples of mislineation.

The difficulties of the compositors printing *Macbeth* did not arise solely from the rhetorical complexities of the verse but also from the technique of printing employed, no doubt aggravated here by complex line-structures. We now know that the Folio was not printed in a simple sequence of pages but simultaneously at different parts of the book – see Charlton Hinman, *The Printing and Proof-reading of the First Folio of Shakespeare* (1963). In order to achieve this, the 'copy' which the printers used had to be marked off in approximate page-lengths, so that when printer A met up with printer B the material would join neatly without gaps or overlaps. The printed form had to be manipulated to fill the space of a page even if the material turned out to be too great or too little. When there was too little material, the compositor would take to 'losing space' by printing in short lines. When he was 'saving space' he joined up lines. Several examples of this seem to be shown in *Macbeth*. The second column of page 136 in the Folio, containing the first forty-seven lines of Act II, scene 2, is jammed full of type. Lines like 'I had most need of Blessing, and Amen stuck in my throat' are pushed right up to the edge of the page. It seems obvious that the compositor is saving space. The same seems to be true on the first page of *Macbeth* in the Folio (I.1 and I.2.1–65).

On the other hand the first column of page 133 (I.3.105–56) is very spaciously laid-out, partly by the device of printing several of the lines in two parts. The compositor clearly was arranging to have the heading for scene 4 at the head of his second column and was prepared to 'misline' to get it there. Other fairly clear examples of 'space-losing' occur on Folio page 138 (II.3.70–II.4.19) and in the second column of page 145 (IV.2.31–85).

I give below a full list of mislineations which have been emended in this edition. The alternative version comes from the Folio. The end of the line in the Folio version is marked by a vertical stroke preceded by the last word of the line; the spelling of the Folio has been preserved; but Elizabethan typographical conventions have been normalized to accord with modern practice. The lay-out is necessarily curt and even cryptic, but the interested reader should be able to reconstruct what has happened in each case and see how far the mislineations fit into the categories outlined above.

I.2.	33–5	Dismayed . . . lion] . . . *Banquoh* | . . . Eagles | . . . Lyon |
	38, 39	So . . . foe] *One line*
	42, 43	I cannot . . . help] . . . faint | . . . helpe |
I.3.	5	And . . . I] And mouncht, & mouncht, and mouncht | . . . I |
	77	With . . . you] . . . greeting | . . . you |
	81	Melted . . . stayed] . . . Winde | . . . stay'd |
	107, 108	The Thane . . . robes] . . . lives | . . . Robes |
	110–13	Which he . . . know not] . . . loose | . . . Norway | . . . helpe | . . . labour'd | . . . not |
	130, 131	Cannot . . . success] . . . good | . . . successe |
	143	If . . . crown me] . . . King | . . . Crowne me |
	149–53	Give . . . time] . . . favour | . . . forgotten | . . .

registred | . . . Leafe | . . . them | . . . upon |
. . . time |

156 Till . . . friends] . . . enough | . . . friends |

I.4. 3–9 My liege . . . died] . . . back | . . . die | . . . hee |
. . . Pardon | . . . Repentance | . . . him | . . .
dy'de |

24–8 In doing . . . honour] . . . selfe | . . . Duties |
. . . State | . . . should | . . . Love | . . . Honor |

I.5. 20, 21 And yet . . have it] . . . winne | . . . cryes | . . .
have it |

I.6. 1, 2 This . . . itselfe] . . . seat | . . . it selfe |

17–20 Against . . . hermits] . . . broad | . . . House |
. . . Dignities | . . . Ermites |

II.1. 4 Hold . . . heaven] . . . Sword | . . . Heaven |

7–9 And yet . . . repose] . . . sleepe | . . . thoughts |
. . repose |

16, 17 By . . . content] . . . Hostesse | . . . content |

25, 26 If you . . . for you] . . . consent | . . . for you |

II.2. 2–6 What . . . possets] . . . fire | . . . shriek'd | . . .
good-night | . . . open | . . . charge | . . . Possets |

14 I . . . noise] . . . deed | . . . noyse |

18, 19 Hark . . . chamber] *One line*

22–5 There's . . . to sleep] . . . sleepe | . . other |
. . . Prayers | . . . to sleepe |

32, 33 I had . . throat] *One line*

65–9 To wear . . . more knocking] . . . white | . . .
entry | . . . Chamber | . . . deed | . . . Constancie |
. . unattended | . . . more knocking |

73, 74 To know . . . couldst] . . . deed | . . . my selfe |
. . . knocking | . . . could'st |

II.3. 22, 23 Faith . . . things] *Two lines of verse:* . . . Cock |
. . things |

48, 49 I'll . . . service] *One line*

51–3 The night . . . death] . . . unruly | . . . downe |
. . . Ayre | . . . Death |

56–8 New-hatched . . . shake] . . . time | . . . Night |
. . . fevorous | . . . shake |

83, 84   O Banquo . . . murdered] *One line*

118-20   What . . . brewed] . . . here | . . . hole | . . away | . . . brew'd |

132   What . . . them] . . . doe | . . . them |

134-8   Which . . . shot] . . . easie | . . . England | . . . I | . . . safer | . . . Smiles | . . . bloody | . . . shot |

II.4.   14   And . . . certain] . . . Horses | . . . certaine |

19, 20   They . . . Macduff] . . . did so | . . . upon't | . . . good *Macduffe* |

III.1. 34, 35   Craving . . . with you] . . . Horse | . . . Night | . . . with you |

41-5   Till . . . pleasure] . . . societie | . . . welcome | . . . alone | . . . with you | . . . men | . . . pleasure |

47-50   Bring . . . dares] . . . us | . . . thus | . . . deepe | . . . that | . . . dares |

71   And . . . there] . . . th'utterance | . . . there |

74-81   Well then . . . might] . . . then | . . . speeches | . . . past | . . . fortune | . . . selfe | . . . conference | . . . you | . . . crost | . . . them | . . . might |

84-90   I did . . . ever] . . . so | . . . now | . . . meeting | . . . predominant | . . . goe | . . . man | . . . hand | . . . begger'd | . . . ever |

113, 114   Both . . . enemy] *One line*

127   Your . . . most] . . . you | . . most |

III.2.   16   But . . . suffer] . . . dis-joynt | . . . suffer |

22   In . . . grave] . . . extasie | . . . Grave |

32, 33   Unsafe . . . streams] . . . lave | . . . streames |

43, 44   Hath . . . note] . . . Peale | . . . note |

III.3.   17   O . . . fly, fly, fly] . . . Trecherie | . . . flye, flye, flye |

III.4.   1, 2   You . . . welcome] . . . downe | . . . welcome |

12, 13   The table . . . face] *One line*

15, 16   My lord . . . him] *One line*

19, 20   Most . . . perfect] . . . Sir | . . scap'd | . . againe | . . . perfect |

47   Here . . highness] . . Lord | . . . Highnesse |

108, 109   You have . . . disorder] . . . mirth | . . . disorder |

	121	It . . . blood will have blood] . . . say | Blood will have Blood |
III.5.	36	Come . . . again] . . . be | . . . againe |
III.6.	1	My . . . thoughts] . . . Speeches | . . . Thoughts |
IV.1.	70	Macbeth, Macbeth, Macbeth . . . Macduff] *Macbeth, Macbeth, Macbeth* | *. . . Macduffe* |
	78	Be . . . scorn] . . . resolute | . . . scorne |
	85, 86	What . . . king] *One line*
IV.2.	27	Fathered he is . . . fatherless] Father'd he is | . . . Father-lesse |
	35, 36	Poor . . . gin] . . . Bird | . . . Lime | . . . Gin |
	37	Why . . . set for] . . . Mother | . . . set for |
	39	Yes . . . father] . . . dead | . . . Father |
	59, 60	Now . . . father] *Verse*: . . . Monkie | . . . Father |
	79	To say . . . faces] . . . harme | . . . faces |
IV.3.	25	Perchance . . . doubts] . . . there | . . . doubts |
	102, 103	Fit . . . miserable] *One line*
	173, 174	Dying . . . grief] . . . sicken | . . . true | . . . griefe |
	211–13	My children . . . killed too] . . . Children too | . . . found | . . . kil'd too |
V.1. 44, 45		Go to, go to . . . not] Go too, go too | . . . not |
V.6.	1	Now . . . down] . . . enough | . . . downe |
	93	Hail . . . stands] . . . art | . . . stands |

READ MORE IN PENGUIN

In every corner of the world, on every subject under the sun, Penguin represents quality and variety – the very best in publishing today.

For complete information about books available from Penguin – including Puffins, Penguin Classics and Arkana – and how to order them, write to us at the appropriate address below. Please note that for copyright reasons the selection of books varies from country to country.

In the United Kingdom: Please write to *Dept. EP, Penguin Books Ltd, Bath Road, Harmondsworth, West Drayton, Middlesex UB7 ODA*

In the United States: Please write to *Consumer Sales, Penguin Putnam Inc., P.O. Box 12289 Dept. B, Newark, New Jersey 07101-5289.* VISA and MasterCard holders call 1-800-788-6262 to order Penguin titles

In Canada: Please write to *Penguin Books Canada Ltd, 10 Alcorn Avenue, Suite 300, Toronto, Ontario M4V 3B2*

In Australia: Please write to *Penguin Books Australia Ltd, P.O. Box 257, Ringwood, Victoria 3134*

In New Zealand: Please write to *Penguin Books (NZ) Ltd, Private Bag 102902, North Shore Mail Centre, Auckland 10*

In India: Please write to *Penguin Books India Pvt Ltd, 11 Community Centre, Panchsheel Park, New Delhi 110017*

In the Netherlands: Please write to *Penguin Books Netherlands bv, Postbus 3507, NL-1001 AH Amsterdam*

In Germany: Please write to *Penguin Books Deutschland GmbH, Metzlerstrasse 26, 60594 Frankfurt am Main*

In Spain: Please write to *Penguin Books S. A., Bravo Murillo 19, 1° B, 28015 Madrid*

In Italy: Please write to *Penguin Italia s.r.l., Via Benedetto Croce 2, 20094 Corsico, Milano*

In France: Please write to *Penguin France, Le Carré Wilson, 62 rue Benjamin Baillaud, 31500 Toulouse*

In Japan: Please write to *Penguin Books Japan Ltd, Kaneko Building, 2-3-25 Koraku, Bunkyo-Ku, Tokyo 112*

In South Africa: Please write to *Penguin Books South Africa (Pty) Ltd, Private Bag X14, Parkview, 2122 Johannesburg*

The Royal Shakespeare Company today is probably one of the best-known theatre companies in the world, playing regularly to audiences of more than a million people a year. The RSC has three theatres in Stratford-upon-Avon, the Royal Shakespeare Theatre, the Swan Theatre and The Other Place, and two theatres in London's Barbican Centre, the Barbican Theatre and The Pit. The Company also has an annual season in Newcastle-upon-Tyne and regularly undertakes tours throughout the UK and overseas.

Find out more about the RSC and its current repertoire by joining the Company's mailing list. Not only will you receive advance information of all the Company's activities, but also priority booking, special ticket offers, copies of the RSC Magazine and special offers on RSC publications and merchandise.

If you would like to receive details of the Company's work and an application form for the mailing list please write to:

RSC Membership Office
Royal Shakespeare Theatre
FREEPOST
Stratford-upon-Avon
CV37 6BR

or telephone: 01789 205301

READ MORE IN PENGUIN

CRITICAL STUDIES

Described by *The Times Educational Supplement* as 'admirable' and 'superb', Penguin Critical Studies is a specially developed series of critical essays on the major works of literature for use by students in universities, colleges and schools.

Titles published or in preparation include:

The Alchemist
The Poetry of William Blake
Critical Theory
Dickens's Major Novels
Doctor Faustus
Dombey and Son
Frankenstein
Great Expectations
The Great Gatsby
Heart of Darkness
The Poetry of Gerard
  Manley Hopkins
The Poetry of Keats
Mansfield Park
The Mayor of Casterbridge

Middlemarch
Paradise Lost
The Poetry of Alexander Pope
Rosencrantz and Guildenstern
  are Dead
Sense and Sensibility
Sons and Lovers
Tennyson
Tess of the D'Urbervilles
To the Lighthouse
The Waste Land
Wordsworth
Wuthering Heights
The Poetry of W. B. Yeats

READ MORE IN PENGUIN

CRITICAL STUDIES

Described by *The Times Educational Supplement* as 'admirable' and 'superb', Penguin Critical Studies is a specially developed series of critical essays on the major works of literature for use by students in universities, colleges and schools.

Titles published or in preparation include:

SHAKESPEARE

As You Like It
Hamlet
King Lear
Macbeth
The Merchant of Venice
A Midsummer Night's Dream
Much Ado about Nothing
Othello
Shakespeare's History Plays
The Taming of the Shrew
The Tempest
Twelfth Night
The Winter's Tale

CHAUCER

Chaucer
The Prologue to
  The Canterbury Tales

READ MORE IN PENGUIN

THE NEW PENGUIN SHAKESPEARE

All's Well That Ends Well	Barbara Everett
Antony and Cleopatra	Emrys Jones
As You Like It	H. J. Oliver
The Comedy of Errors	Stanley Wells
Coriolanus	G. R. Hibbard
Hamlet	T. J. B. Spencer
Henry IV, Part 1	P. H. Davison
Henry IV, Part 2	P. H. Davison
Henry V	A. R. Humphreys
Henry VI, Parts 1–3	Norman Sanders
(three volumes)	
Henry VIII	A. R. Humphreys
Julius Caesar	Norman Sanders
King John	R. L. Smallwood
King Lear	G. K. Hunter
Love's Labour's Lost	John Kerrigan
Macbeth	G. K. Hunter
Measure for Measure	J. M. Nosworthy
The Merchant of Venice	W. Moelwyn Merchant
The Merry Wives of Windsor	G. R. Hibbard
A Midsummer Night's Dream	Stanley Wells
Much Ado About Nothing	R. A. Foakes
The Narrative Poems	Maurice Evans
Othello	Kenneth Muir
Pericles	Philip Edwards
Richard II	Stanley Wells
Richard III	E. A. J. Honigmann
Romeo and Juliet	T. J. B. Spencer
The Sonnets *and* A Lover's Complaint	John Kerrigan
The Taming of the Shrew	G. R. Hibbard
The Tempest	Anne Barton
Timon of Athens	G. R. Hibbard
Troilus and Cressida	R. A. Foakes
Twelfth Night	M. M. Mahood
The Two Gentlemen of Verona	Norman Sanders
The Two Noble Kinsmen	N. W. Bawcutt
The Winter's Tale	Ernest Schanzer